THE SONG OF THE STORK

As the Second World War burns through Europe, a fifteen-year-old Jewish girl is on the run in the Polish countryside, having narrowly escaped the German soldiers. Now Yael is alone, with only the memory of her brother Josef — fighting with the Red Army far away — to sustain her. Desperate and determined, she seeks shelter on the farm of the village outcast. Aleksei is mute and solitary, and wary of hiding a Jew. But, as the brutal winter advances, he reluctantly takes her in . . . and a delicate relationship begins to flourish between them in their private sanctuary.

STEPHAN COLLISHAW

◆

THE SONG OF THE STORK

Complete and Unabridged

ULVERSCROFT
Leicester

First published in Great Britain in 2017 by
Legend Press Ltd
London

First Large Print Edition
published 2017
by arrangement with
Legend Press Ltd
London

A catalogue record for this book is available
from the British Library.

ISBN 978–1–4448–3441–3

Published by
F. A. Thorpe (Publishing)
Anstey, Leicestershire

Set by Words & Graphics Ltd.
Anstey, Leicestershire
Printed and bound in Great Britain by
T. J. International Ltd., Padstow, Cornwall

This book is printed on acid-free paper

For Marija

1

They left the barn as soon as it was dark. Rivka had stood by the door watching as the light faded, moving from one foot to the other, anxious. When, finally, the shadows were deep enough, they slipped out, ears straining for sounds, stepping bare foot on the gravel, fear numbing the pain of the sharp stones that bit into the soft flesh of the soles of their feet.

The turned earth of the harvested fields was cool and soft after the gravel, but it was heavy going and they were tired before they had crossed halfway towards the forest that lipped the hilltop. Rivka coughed continuously into her sleeve, fearing the sound would travel back across the field.

They sank down when they reached the forest's edge. The moon had just risen and the field shone, illuminated. Rivka's face looked drawn.

'You're bleeding,' Yael whispered, and reaching out wiped the streak of dark blood from her lips with the cuff of her sleeve.

'I must have bitten my lip,' Rivka said.

'But look at your jacket,' Yael pointed at the

dark stain in the crook of her arm, into which Rivka had been coughing.

'Come on, we must move.'

Rivka hauled herself up and turned towards the darkness of the woods.

'We must move as fast as we can.'

Yael followed behind Rivka, arms in front, shielding her face against the supple pine branches that snapped back ferociously as Rivka pushed through them.

★ ★ ★

They covered no more than a couple of miles that night. Exhausted, they found a deep patch of undergrowth and wriggled into the centre of it, the brambles scratching at their faces, bloodying the backs of their hands and calves. Rivka fell asleep almost immediately. For some time, Yael watched her. Her body was emaciated, her cheeks sunken, the skin around her eyes loose and dark. Dried blood flecked her pale lips. Her hands looked like the hands of an old woman. Her breathing was fast, feverish. Her chest rose in a shallow, rapid rhythm. Yael sank down beside her, pulling her close. Covered their bodies with twigs and bracken. Rivka seemed to have shrunk. She was no longer the larger-than-life young woman Yael had first seen on the stage of the House of Culture in Selo, part of the young Yiddish theatre group.

* ★ ★ ★

Or perhaps, Yael thought, I've grown. She lifted her head and surveyed her own body. She too had grown thinner, but her body did not bear the same marks of sickness Rivka's did. Her skin, she noted, was healthy-looking still, tight against her flesh. Her hair was thick, in fact uncomfortably so. She was tempted to take Rivka's knife and chop it off. It lay matted and itchy against the back of her neck.

Her skin was broken by an endless pattern of dried scabs where she had scratched at bites. She had begun to get used to the continual torment of the lice. Rivka had taken a cigarette lighter one day and forced Yael to undress. She had run the flame slowly up each seam. The lice crackled as they fried.

The night was cold and by morning a thick mist had gathered close to the earth. Yael shivered through the dark hours, her body pulled close against Rivka's, which seemed hot. She was, Yael realised, running a temperature. As the light began to seep through the brambles, Rivka began to shake. Her forehead was burning and her clothes were damp, not only with the cold mist, but with sweat.

'Rivka,' Yael whispered into her ear.

The older woman muttered and turned, but did not open her eyes.

'We need to go back to the farm,' Yael said.

But Rivka did not respond. Yael tried to lift her, but was unable to do so. Pushing out of the brambles she wandered around for a while and finally found a small stream. She cupped her hands and drank some water and then looked around for something to carry water back for Rivka, but there was nothing. In the end she took off her blouse, from beneath the man's jacket. She coiled the blouse and dipped it in the water until it was soaked. She carried it back and twisted it gently above Rivka's lips. The water ran from her lips down her face, dirty. She held a corner of the cold wet cloth against Rivka's fevered forehead.

For the rest of the day she sat like that, moving occasionally to bathe the blouse in the stream. There were berries in the brambles and she picked and ate them. She tried to get Rivka to eat, but she was unwilling.

As night fell, Rivka seemed to improve. She opened her eyes and half sat up, leaning against Yael.

'I'm sorry,' she muttered. 'I'm so sorry.'

'Don't be silly,' Yael said, stroking her skin with the damp cool cloth of her blouse. 'You'll be better soon.'

'Yes.' Rivka smiled weakly and tried to pull herself up higher. She ate some berries Yael crushed between her lips and drank some water from the twisted wet blouse on her tongue.

★ ★ ★

When Yael woke the next morning, Rivka felt cooler by her side. She reached across and touched the skin of her forehead with the back of her fingers. The temperature had definitely gone. She sat up.

'Rivka,' she whispered, and shook her softly.

Her body was stiff.

'Rivka?' Yael called, her throat constricting.

Rivka's eyes were closed. When Yael turned her over, she found blood congealed at the corner of her mouth and in the rim of her nostrils. She looked astonishingly calm and it struck Yael, as she gazed at her in disbelief, that it had been a long time since she had seen her face look so calm.

For the rest of morning she sat silently beside Rivka's body, holding her cold hand. A hard lump pressed at her throat but she did not cry.

Later she covered the body with a thick layer of leaves and fronds of fern that were dark green and succulent. She laid them deeply, until there was no hint a body was there. Then she crawled out from the brambles and turned back towards Czeslaw's farm.

2

Standing at the edge of the fields, shaded by the thick branches of the fir trees, Yael stood gazing down on the farm. The yard was thick with German military vehicles and soldiers milled around the barn and the house. Camouflaged tents were erected around the edge of the field. She heard shouts and the sound of laughter. The farmer mingled with the soldiers, passing around bottles. Smoke from a fire rose steadily into the cool still air. She and Rivka had left just in time.

Yael turned and pushed back through the branches into the wood. She wandered aimlessly. She had no idea where she might turn. For some time she sat on the rotting trunk of a fallen tree, head in hands. She considered going back to the *shtetl*, but knew that would be madness. From her pocket she took Rivka's handgun. She ran her fingers along the cold metal barrel, turned it and placed the muzzle of it against the soft skin between her eyes. She could just rest her finger now against the thin trigger and that would be it, she thought. She felt an icy shiver across her skin. She put it away quickly.

Getting up, she wandered away from the farm.

'Oh Josef,' she muttered to herself, thinking of her brother who she had not seen in a year now. 'Where are you?'

From the position of the pale risen sun, she orientated herself and began to make her way northeast in the direction of the Russian front. She had little idea how far the Germans had managed to press the Soviets back. Perhaps they had already won the war, she thought. Perhaps the Russians had admitted defeat.

But she pictured Josef in Red Army uniform on the back of his horse. Never, she thought. He would never admit defeat. There would be more like him.

A couple of miles north, the forest ended suddenly. A dirt road wound down into a low valley. In the centre of the small valley stood a dilapidated farmhouse, with tumbling outbuildings leaned against it. She recognised where she was, though she had only seen the farm once, from the back of a cart that had brought her from the train station in Grodno.

The farm belonged to Aleksei, the idiot. 'He's not crazy,' she remembered her father saying as they bumped along the road, after their trip to Warsaw. 'He just doesn't like company.'

'He doesn't speak,' her mother had said, as if that fact alone was enough to prove his madness.

'And that makes him a *meshúgener?*' her father had retorted. 'Then give me more of them! Give me a whole *shtetl* of *meshúgener!* I could live in such a place.'

Every village had somebody that was crazy. The odd ones. In Selo they had Able. Able had the mind of a child, though his beard was long and his hair beginning to grey. He was a simple and pleasant man who begged for sweets outside the shop and cried when the boys from the town made fun of him. One of Yael's sweetest memories of her brother was the time he had chased off Marek Wolniewicz and his friends who had been tormenting Able. He had gone to the shop and bought some boiled sweets which Able had received with pitiful joy. The thought of it now stabbed her heart with a small pain of longing for the company of her brother.

And then there was Aleksei. His father died when he was a teenager. The story in the village was that he had never spoken, that he had some medical problem that rendered him mute, but there were some who thought differently.

'He spoke as child,' Myra Koppelman asserted. 'I remember visiting his poor mother when he was a toddler and he talked all right then. It was her dying in the way she did that stopped his mouth.'

'That's rubbish,' her husband Eli Koppelman argued. 'He never spoke a word in his life. He isn't able. He has a problem. Doctor Sonenson told me.'

'Sonenson? What does he know?'

Everybody had assumed that when his father died some relative would come and take the teenager, or that he would be sent to live in one of the hostels, but he had refused to move from the farm. He carried on working there, eking out a subsistence from his fields, occasionally trading vegetables or a pig for some goods he could not produce himself. He kept to himself and rarely came to the village, preferring to deal with the couple of nearby farmers he trusted.

* * *

She settled down in the woods, not far from the farm and waited for darkness.

3

There were no lights burning in the windows of the small farm at the foot of the hill. The valley walls seemed to move in with the setting of the sun, so that it grew darker and more secluded. It was only as the day ended, as darkness wound its fingers through the woods, that she began to feel utterly alone.

The fear gripped her. For an hour she crouched, frozen to the spot. She dared not move back into the depths of the woods, which were now pitch black and alive with the noise of animals and birds rooting in the undergrowth, nor step out into the brittle light of the rising moon onto the dirt path for fear she would be seen.

The tears she had not been able to shed when Rivka died came now, suddenly, and for some time refused to stop. But they were not just for Rivka, nor indeed for any of the dead. They were also for herself. Nobody knows where I am she thought, and then, almost immediately, there is nobody left to know who I am. To know I am gone. And then the thought of Josef gave her a renewed sense of determination. He would come back. He will rescue me.

The very image of Josef riding down these country lanes, at the head of a battalion of Soviet soldiers, filled her with strength. I'm all he has left, she thought. I must keep myself safe for him. The idea of Josef returning to the village to find the whole family gone broke her heart. She had to find a way through this.

She stood up, her legs stiff from having squatted for so long. Slowly she eased herself through the last straggle of tree trunks and paused in the deep grass on the verge of the dirt road. The road curved away behind the woods and on towards Selo, passing as it did, Czeslaw's farm, then up, to where the road topped the hill heading from Grodno, a town barely larger than Selo, but with a station from which trains ran directly to Vilna and Warsaw and Minsk. The valley was deserted.

She stepped out into the moonlight. Crossing the road and the field quickly, she made her way to the farmhouse. The grass was high and the earth uneven. She walked with care, moving slowly, stopping often to listen and to examine the farmhouse for signs of life. There was little evidence anybody lived in the farm. No light. No smoke curling from the chimney.

Perhaps he is gone, she thought. Perhaps

he has fled north to Russia. Or perhaps, like others, he has welcomed the Germans and gone to live in the town, believing it to be safer under their protection.

Perhaps he is dead, she thought too, crouching in the long grass, the seed-heavy heads motionless above her. She strained to see the details of the dark windows, to catch a glimpse of movement behind the dusty glass. She recalled the face of Rivka, her white lips, the hollowness of her face, as if death had sucked away her flesh as well as her spirit.

The evening silence was broken by a shout. A sharp shriek that seemed to echo around her. From the corner of her eye she caught a movement. She flattened down against the earth, her heart hammering. Glancing up a few moments later she could see nothing. Holding her breath, she listened intently. The grass whispered. Then she heard it again, in the distance now, towards the bank of trees rising up on the west of the valley and she saw the owl silhouetted against the last traces of sunset. She slowly released her breath. Struggling to calm her racing heart.

Crawling forward on hands and knees she found, at last, the dirt path that wound down the hill to the farmhouse. Straightening up she walked down it cautiously, but when she got close to the building, she cut off and circled around, keeping to the shade of the trees.

The house was silent. It was wooden, as were all but the most substantial houses in the town and its environs. Closed shutters masked many of the windows. The glass was dirty and opaque on those that were visible. At the back of the house an old barrel caught water from the guttering. A well stood at the bottom of the garden, an overturned bucket by its side.

No dog barked. Nobody coughed. The silence was deafening.

Yael moved forward on hands and knees. She was hungry and thirsty. There was no sign the mute was in the house, and if he was, she reasoned, he must surely have been sleeping.

She lowered the bucket into the well slowly, ensuring it did not knock against the brick sides. It was a finely constructed well, neat and maintained. The bucket was wooden, secured with metal straps. It was heavy to pull up when filled with water, and she struggled as the rope cut against her fingers.

Lowering the bucket to the floor, she dipped her hands into it and drank deeply. The water was cold and fresh, sweet to her parched mouth. It dripped musically from her fingers. The night pulsed with the sound of grasshoppers. When she had drunk enough, she emptied the water onto the grass and laid the bucket as she had found it.

At the far end of the grassed yard stood a rickety hencoop. Listening for any sounds of disturbance, she crept towards the coop. The hens grumbled as she squeezed through the entrance, one squawking with fright, fearing perhaps it was a fox or a wolf. But after a few minutes, sensing there was no danger, it settled again.

The hencoop was no more than two metres in length. A couple of shelves on either side served as perches. Yael gathered straw and curled herself in the far corner beneath a shelf, covering herself as best she could, knees drawn up against her chest, her skirt pulled tight around her.

After the nights in the forest, the hencoop seemed luxurious. She had forgotten what it had been like to lie in a bed. She tried to imagine. Tried to recall how life had been before it had been so brutally and so comprehensively torn from its path. She found it hard to recall the contours of her home, to bring to mind, even, the face of her mother. She pictured her father beside her, at the door of their house, tacks sticking from between his lips, like rotten teeth. 'A still small voice,' he said. 'It was not in the

15

thunder nor the lightning, nor in the strong wind, but in the still small voice that God was.' But she realised he could not have said that then, if his mouth had been full of tacks.

When she slept, she dreamt of her father. He was dressed in black and surrounded by her uncles. A melancholy chant filled the air. The men rose around her like crows. The noise filled the air, the rustling of wings. *Yisgadal v'yiskadash shmey rabo.* The room was hot. She was squeezed in the corner. In the centre of the room, not visible, her grandfather lay in his coffin on the table. *B'olmo divro khirusey v'yamlikh malkhusey.* The wings beat hard around her, the black shadows flickered, arms or wings pounding, rising up out of the branches of the trees, the light opening up above them, pouring down into the room. *B'khayeykheyn uvyeymeykheyn uv'khayey d'khol Beys Yisróel . . .*

And with the name Israel, the room exploded with light, as the crows soared up into the air and she awoke to see a head pushing in through the door of the hencoop and the hens all aflutter and the sunlight brilliant through the cracks in the wooden panelling.

4

He had gone before she registered who it was. The image of an arm snaking in through the doorway lingered in her mind. The rustle of hens settled slowly in her ears. She sat up sharply, narrowly avoiding banging her head against a shelf. On her hands and knees she pressed her face to the crack beside the door through which light flooded.

Aleksei walked up the path towards the house. In his hands he carried eggs. He paused at the threshold and looked up into the sky, as if he had perhaps heard something. Yael saw his chest expand as he inhaled deeply. He glanced around and for a moment his eyes rested upon the hencoop and she wondered if he had seen her. He turned then and disappeared into the darkness.

Yael sat back and rested her head against the wooden wall. Her stomach was tight with hunger. Her throat burned. She needed a drink. Twice she steeled herself to crawl out through the low narrow door and go up to the farmhouse, but found at the last moment she could not.

Later she heard him moving around at the

back of the house. She pressed her eye against the crack and watched as he split logs.

The mute looked as though he was in his twenties. He had dark, beautiful hair that fell against his bare shoulders and reminded her, for some reason, of her old school friend Eva's. The day was crisp and fresh, the sky cloudless. The sun was distant though, and in the shadows it was cold. The mute worked up a sweat chopping the logs and storing them neatly against the side of the house. On the floor, by the side of the stacked logs, lay a tarpaulin, and when he had finished he pulled it across them.

For some minutes he stood outside the back of his house, leaning against the winter fuel. He wiped his chest with the shirt he had been wearing and draped it around his shoulders. From his back pocket he took out a cigarette packet and extracted one and lit it. He surveyed the short field that stretched down from the back of the house. His eyes rested again on the hencoop and Yael drew back from the slit in the wall and sat trembling on her haunches.

It was dark when finally she emerged. A light burned faintly in a downstairs window of the house. She crawled from the hencoop to the well and lowered the bucket down into the darkness. She struggled more than she had the previous night when she tried to pull it back up full. Her head throbbed and she was faint with hunger.

As soon as the sun had set, it began to grow cold and she shivered as she dipped her head to sip from the bucket. The water revived her a little. She sat with her back to the brick wall. Her head spun. Touching her forehead she found that it was hot, despite the coldness of the night. The fear she would develop the fever that had killed Rivka forced her to her feet.

Unsteadily she walked towards the farm-house. She stepped carefully, avoiding making a noise that would raise attention. The window of the kitchen was so thick with dust, and the light that illuminated the room so faint, she had to wipe it softly in order to see inside.

He was seated at a large table in the centre of the room. He had his back to the window and was bent forward motionless. On the table before him stood a candle. Its flame flickered slightly. At his elbow a plate lay, with the leftovers of his supper: shards of an eggshell and the remains of a thick crust.

He sat in complete stillness. It was only after a few minutes, when he moved, that Yael saw he had been reading.

He stood and carried the plate towards the

window. Yael dodged back. She heard his feet on the floorboards. The door creaked. She pressed herself tight against the wall. He appeared in the doorway and in his hand he carried his supper plate. He threw the crusts out into the grass and turned back, immediately closing the door behind him.

When Yael stood up, some minutes later, the candle had been extinguished. She peered through the window, but could see nobody. She found the crusts on the grass and folded them into her palm. She found too some of the brittle shards of eggshell. She put one of these against her tongue. The taste of the egg, or perhaps just its scent, flooded her mouth, so that saliva spilt out over her chapped lips.

After drinking some more water from the bucket she crawled back inside the hencoop and settled down in the straw with the bread crusts. Despite the hunger, she forced herself to bite off minute portions, making sure she lost no crumbs, and allowed the hard crust to soften on her tongue, savouring it, or crushing it gently between her teeth, so the full flavour burst out and filled her mouth. Never had bread tasted so good.

Though the crusts by no means satisfied her hunger, she slept better that night. The proximity of the hens, the straw and the shelter of the coop kept her warm. She gave into sleep easily. This time, undisturbed by vivid dreams.

The morning was a cold one and when she peeped out between the slats in the wooden panelling she could see the first thick frost had settled across the grass. A thin column of smoke rose from the chimney of the farmhouse and hung in the sky. It was early, the sun had still not risen and the light was ghostly pale. Yael wrapped her arms around herself. She tried holding one of the hens to keep her warm, but it struggled too much and pecked at her arms and she was forced to let it settle back on its perch. Returning the hen, she found an egg. Touching it, she felt its warmth. Glancing out through the slats once more, she saw no movement. A solitary crow rested on the roof tiles.

Settling back on the straw in the corner, she cradled the egg in the palm of her hand. Its shell was smooth. She held it to her lips, feeling its faint warmth, inhaling the scent. Then very carefully she tapped the full rounded end against the corner of one of the shelves. She tapped it very delicately until the shell showed the first signs of a hairline crack, then with the tips of her fingernails, she eased off a small chip of shell and sucked out the egg.

It was not the first time that she had done

this. Her brother Josef had shown her how to suck an egg, piercing it with one of the tacks their father used for mending shoes, when she was no more than four. They had emptied five eggs between them, from her mother's pantry, replacing each one seemingly intact. When their mother had discovered what had happened she had flown into a rage. Yael had watched as their father reluctantly punished Josef. Their mother did not suspect Yael had been involved and Josef did not breathe a word. She went to him afterwards as he lay smarting on his bed, but he simply turned his head so she would not see he had been crying.

The thought of it now hurt her more than was rational. She pictured the way he looked at her as he shared the illicit meal, the joy she had felt from that beautiful complicity. And how useless and rejected she had felt as he turned his tear-stained face from her. The way he had shuffled away as she tried to touch his hair the way her father did when she was hurt.

Crouching down, she eased herself out of the hencoop before Aleksei rose and was in the woods when he emerged from the house and trudged down to collect his eggs.

In the woods she found some late berries, shrivelled and touched by frost. She ate them greedily, savouring each one on her tongue for as long as she could, to eke out the moment of pleasure.

Turning back to the farm, she crawled around to the vegetable patch and broke off the leaves from some cabbage, which were bitter and almost inedible. In a compost heap she found the fresh scattered bones of a cooked chicken, and the peel of some potatoes. She ate the peel and gnawed on the bones, the fat and blood lubricating her lips and dripping down her chin.

The beggar's breakfast filled her with enough courage to determine to approach the mute. Still the hours passed and she watched him from among the trees as he chopped more wood and then climbed up onto the roof of the house and nailed into place some loose tiles.

The sun was falling in the late afternoon when he finally got down and Yael stood up, unsteadily. She breathed in deeply and stepped forward. He did not see her until she was almost at the bottom of the path, thirty yards away. He looked up startled. Yael hesitated. She stumbled, tripping over her own feet and fell to her knees. It was only then the mute seemed to recognise her. She saw the look pass over his face.

She got up and approached him. He stood

as if rooted to the spot, in his hand the hammer and tacks he had been using to repair the roof for winter. She stopped some yards from him. Her hands were clasped together tightly to stop them from shaking. For some moments they stood in silence before each other. A rooster bellowed from the roof of the hencoop and in the distance Yael heard a dog barking. She searched for the right thing to say.

'I have nowhere to go,' she said finally, simply. She could feel his eyes upon her. She could not raise her own. Each time she tried to do so, it was as though the sight of him blinded her.

He did not answer. Yael could hear the sound of his breathing, heavy, jagged intakes of breath. A ripple of fear ran across her skin, raising goose pimples. She wiped her face nervously with the back of her hand and noticed the blood and grease from the chicken smudged across it.

'Shelter me,' she pleaded, her voice small and reticent.

She heard him move. Glancing up she saw he was sweating. He stepped from one foot to the other, the hammer trembling in his hand.

'Please,' she whispered in Polish. She moved a little closer to him, so close she could smell him. He smelled warm, earthy, like an animal. Not unpleasant.

He muttered something. When she looked up again, he was shaking his head. The hammer slipped from his grasp and fell to the earth. A hard, guttural hiss escaped from his throat. He shook his head hard. Turning, he dashed into the house. For a moment Yael stood startled. As she was considering moving towards the doorway, though, he re-emerged. In his hand he held a piece of folded paper.

He thrust the sheet at her. It was crinkled and smudged and at first she could not decipher the writing. The top part she found was written in German, in an ornate gothic script. *Attention!* it read. She could not understand the rest, picking out only the word *Juden*.

The mute's finger stabbed at the lower half of the page. Yael folded the paper down and found the text had been translated into Polish. It was badly translated and the typeset used to print it was crude and careless. She read it swiftly. Her heart quickened and she felt her face flush. The Jews were filthy vermin, it stated simply, and anybody found guilty of harbouring them, feeding them or in any way aiding them would be summarily executed.

She glanced up at Aleksei. His face was creased with worry. Fear. His hand shook as he took back the sheet of paper. He pointed to the word *Juden* and then at Yael. He then ran his finger across his throat and made a strange, strangulated noise. The action did not scare Yael. She pitied him and the position she had put him in. He seemed, as he stood before her in silent, wordless supplication, no more than a boy. A small, frightened child.

'Nobody would know,' she whispered. Then, emboldened, 'I would hide. I wouldn't go out.'

His eyes widened. He shook his head vigorously.

'Please,' she pleaded.

This seemed to infuriate him. He stabbed at the paper, his finger jabbing so hard it ripped through the sheet. He made several cutting motions at his throat again. He reached out and pushed her away. His touch was not aggressive, but it was firm and clear in its intent. Yael stumbled. She fell to her knees before him and raised her hands.

'I beg . . . '

The mute reached down and grabbed her arm. He pulled her up roughly and propelled her along the path before him. Yael tried to twist out of his grip, to turn and talk to him, but he held her too tightly.

He marched her up off the farm and

pushed her out into the dirt road. When she turned to him he seemed for a moment to be at a loss as to what to do, but reaching down he picked up a stick from the side of the road and brandished it at her. His lips worked and she heard strange noises working their way up from his chest. She was not sure whether they were coughs, or a faltering roar. She was half caught between her fear of him and pity for him in his fear.

At last she withdrew. She stumbled across the road and fell down at the edge of the woods. For some minutes they faced each other on opposite sides of the road. Tears slid down her filthy face. He, on the other side, waved his stick, muttering and barking like a frightened dog.

He turned and walked slowly down the path towards his house. Occasionally he stopped to check she was not following him. Each time he raised his stick and shook it. When at last he disappeared inside the house, Yael knew he was watching from behind the dark glass.

5

She did not hide when later she went back to the hencoop. She had stayed for an hour by the side of the road, her chin rested upon her knees, gazing down at the small farm. She saw his face behind the dirty glass, looking out. Often he ran his hand through his thick hair and down across his face.

She stood hesitantly. The sun hung over the trees, distant and wintry, its thin light dying before it had even managed to set. A frosty mist rose from the earth. Her whole body convulsed with shivers and no matter how much she stamped her feet, or wrapped her arms around herself, or blew against her fingers, she could feel no relief from the gnawing, damp cold.

Slowly she stepped forward across the gravel road and stood on the edge of his land. She stopped there a while and waited to see what he would do. His face was ghostly behind the window. She moved another pace and then another. Like a dog edging its way towards the fire, unsure whether it would get there, or if it would be kicked away. When he did not move, she grew in confidence and walked down the path, passing by the side of the house, by the well, across the back field to the hencoop.

She turned before she pushed through the flap into its relative shelter. He had come around to the back of the house and watched. She met his eyes. For a number of seconds they regarded each other, eye to eye, and she could not tell who was more afraid.

The night was cold. The mist seeped through the cracks between the boards. When she woke in the middle of the night, the trail of saliva from her mouth had frozen lightly on the collar of her jacket. She curled up into a tight ball, every bone aching, every muscle painful, shaking with cold.

God take me, she thought as her eyes closed again heavily. Or spare me if you will. And she did not know which to pray for, that she may not wake again, or that she would survive the night.

When she woke it was light, a thin luminosity, mean and unwelcoming. She lay still, unable to move. Thick crust had sealed her left eye and she could see little with her right. She listened to the shuffle of the hens. Their low clucking soothed her. She knew that it was only a matter of time. Fever would take her, or the cold, or hunger. Perhaps he, the mute, would betray her to the police.

29

Perhaps already he had gone down to the town to notify them there was *vermin* on his farm. She found she did not care.

She passed in and out of sleep. Sleeping she dreamed fevered, suffocating dreams she struggled to be free from, but when she woke, the pain in her head and her body and the cold so tortured her she longed once more for sleep.

At one point, she was aware that a face appeared above her and wildly she murmured her brother's name.

'Josef?'

The air barely stirred from her lips and the face disappeared. When she woke next she felt warmer. Her sleep had been less fitful and she felt a slight easing of the pain in her body. She turned and realised she had been covered with something. Rising, she found an old cover had been laid carefully across her. She pulled it tight and slipped once more into darkness, this time solid and deep, so when she woke finally it was with a gasp, as if she had risen from some deep hole, or from the depths of the sea, or in fact, from death itself.

Yael sat up, picked the crust from her eyes and gazed about blearily. It was barely light, but she could not tell whether it was morning or evening. She gathered the corners of the blanket around her and leaned back against the wooden boards of the hencoop.

He brought me a blanket, she thought.

'Thank you,' she whispered, the words steaming pleasantly on the bare skin of her hands. Almost instantly her eyes fell on the paper lying on the floor of the hencoop close to the door. Without needing to read it, she recognised the ornate gothic script, the poor print. *Juden. Vermin.*

Coming as it did, after the kindness of the blanket, Yael found herself not afraid, nor hurt, but rather angry. She felt a fury mounting within her. Fury at the author who had misspelled *szkodniki*, at the typesetter who had done his job incompetently, at the arrogance of the Germans, at the mute for bringing her the blanket and this warning. She shuffled forwards, holding the blanket tight around her and poked her feet through the door of the hencoop.

It was evening. The sky was covered with a dark, thick smear of cloud. The air was damp with rain, but warmer than it had been. Candle-light illuminated the kitchen window faintly. Boldly, Yael trudged up the path, her feet soaking in the thick grass and stood at the closed door of the house. She paused and took a deep breath. Her heart was pumping and her hand trembled as she lifted it and rapped on the door so hard her knuckles hurt.

6

From the other side of the door Yael heard a sound. The scuffing of feet on bare boards. She stood back a pace, expecting the door to spring open, but it did not. After a few moments she stepped forward and knocked again, more gently this time, not because she was less determined, but because her thin, pale knuckles ached from the previous blow.

He stood on the other side of the wood and she could hear his breathing, laboured, hard, frightened. He cleared his throat continuously. She rested her head against the central panel and listened to him.

'Open it,' she whispered. Then louder, more stridently, 'Open the door.'

There was a short pause and the clearing of his throat ceased. I've scared him now, she thought, but a moment later she heard a movement and the door handle turned. She stood back and watched as it opened a fraction. His eye appeared in the gap. He stood as a small child might, left alone in his home, answering the door to a stranger. At once Yael felt the anger subsiding in her, replaced by a whisper of pity.

'I'm hungry,' she said.

He looked out at her, not moving. The door opened no wider, but also it did not close and for that Yael was thankful; it bore in her a splinter of hope, a morsel of comfort.

'Please,' she whispered through the gap.

He pressed the door closed carefully, quietly.

She stood looking at its sudden blankness, unsure of what would follow. She heard his feet move away and realised no bolts had been shot, no key had been turned in the lock. She could, she thought, push open the door and walk in.

When the mute opened the door again, he opened it wider. Yael's eyes flicked over his shoulder and scanned the room. It was a simple kitchen, a table in its centre, solid and large. On the table stood a candle, by the side of it a book, upturned so the pages fanned out against the rough wood. The candle was not lit yet and the room was shrouded in the oncoming darkness of evening.

Into her hands he pushed a small bundle, a paper bag. She grasped it and pulled it close against her body without looking at it. He turned away immediately and closed the door, quietly, gently, but firmly.

Yael turned and walked back to the hencoop. Inside, in the twilight, she opened the bag and pulled out some dark rye bread and a lump of cheese. Something cold touched her fingertips and reaching to the bottom of the bag she found a short, sharp knife.

She did not use the knife to slice the bread and cheese into neat sandwiches, as perhaps he imagined she might, but bit hungrily into the crust of bread and quickly devoured all of it, along with the cheese. The hunger was too consuming for her to be patient. Her stomach hurt when she had finished. She retched and thought she was going to be sick. She put her hands across her mouth as if to keep the little sustenance within her, as if she might force it back down should it come up.

Later she curled up, pulling the blanket tight around her. From the inside of the jacket she wore, she took out a photograph she had taken from her bedroom and placed it on the dirty floor of the hencoop before her. Josef stood tall and handsome in the photographer's studio at the end of Warsaw Street. His hand rested on the back of an empty chair, the other shoved nonchalantly into the pocket of his trousers. His suit was sharply cut, she noticed, his hair neatly combed back, just the faintest hint of the wisp of an unruly curl attempting to break free and fall across his high forehead. The corner of his lips was turned up in a grin.

'Josef,' she murmured, kissing the torn and creased photograph gently. 'Don't forget me Josef. Come back for me.' She did not doubt he would. That faith burned irrepressibly in her bosom. He would not forget her, she knew, she believed with her whole heart. He would come on the back of a horse, smart in his Red Army uniform. He would save her.

★   ★   ★

The next morning Yael woke to find the mute had left a cup of milk and crust of bread just inside the door of the coop. Though the night had been cold, the blanket had kept the sharpness of it off and she had managed to sleep fairly well.

She ate the crust of bread and drank the milk less hastily, taking pleasure in their taste, and when she had finished she did not feel sick. The strength, she could feel, was beginning to return to her limbs. She had recently been suffering sharp shooting pains whenever she flexed a limb or moved her head too quickly. But movement was a little easier too.

Later she pulled a bucket of water from the well and took it into the forest. She stripped away some of the layers of clothes and bathed herself as best she could. Using her fingers, she tidied her hair and plaited it loosely but as neatly as she could. It had grown longer over the summer and autumn months. As she washed herself, she could see just how much her body had changed. She could see the bones, angular and ugly, jutting out almost piercing her pale, transparent skin. She traced a finger along her ribs.

★ ★ ★

The mute left her some more food at the end of the day. She was aware he watched her nervously. He seemed content so long as she did not approach the house or show herself too visibly. That was perhaps why he brought her the food, she thought, to keep her from knocking on his door again. To keep her from coming out looking for it.

For some days they lived like that. Yael hid for the most part in the hencoop, venturing out only to draw water, or occasionally to walk in the deep stretch of woods behind the house where there was little chance of her being seen. Aleksei would leave her food, morning and evening; bread, occasionally cheese, once the end of a sausage, pork which she agonised over for a day before the scent of it overcame her reluctance and she ate it, finding the meat difficult to swallow, not just because of her anxiety and repugnance, but because it was chewy and hard and did not dissolve in her mouth as the bread did, or disintegrate like the cheese.

She began to think they could last like that, though the weather was growing colder by the day, and there had even been a hint of snow. She found a store of hay in a side shed, whilst out exploring one evening. She had taken to moving around after darkness. Cautiously she would approach the house window and watch him sat there with a book, reading by the light of a candle stub. Once she was sure he was occupied, she felt safe to move around. The shed door had been difficult to open, the bolt having rusted. Inside it was dark and dry. The room was well sealed and warmer than the hencoop and she considered staying there, but worried it might prompt the mute to attempt to get rid of her again.

Pressing the door open as wide as it would go, she felt around, seeing more with the tips of her fingers than with her eyes. On a shelf she discovered a stack of what she took to be books, thick with dust. In the corner she found hay, brittle, dry and old. She took an embrace full and stuffed it through the small door of the hencoop, returning for more. When she had pressed three arms full into the coop, she quietly closed the door of the shed and attempted to slide back the bolt. It was too difficult though and all she could manage was to edge the tip into the metal ring on the doorframe, enough to stop it from swinging open in the breeze.

That night she worried the mute would discover the drawn bolt the next morning. She slept fitfully, despite being warmer in the bed of hay. When she woke, it was later than usual and fully light. A noise had pulled her from a dream of Rivka. She lay still for some moments, the image of the woman's face drifting across the closed lids of her eyes. A voice startled her. It was close, not more than a few feet from the hencoop.

She sat up sharply, her heart thumping. Before she even pressed her face to the crack between the boards she knew it was German soldiers.

7

The mute stood by the door of his house. His dark hair stood out wildly from the sides of his head, as though he had been dragged from his bed, his chin was rough with stubble and his eyes wide. He wore dark trousers, but the belt, Yael noticed, hung loose and his shirt was unbuttoned. She saw at once he had not betrayed her to the Nazis.

There were six or seven smartly dressed German soldiers. They milled around the farm, opening doors, calling crisp commands. A large, fair-haired soldier had slid back the bolt of the outhouse from which Yael had fetched hay the previous evening. Looking out now, through the narrow gaps between the boards, Yael noticed the thin trace of hay she had trailed across the field.

The morning was dry, but the sky overcast. Large clouds moved south, stained and heavy. Snow was imminent. At the top of the path Yael noticed a civilian, a poorly dressed man in his mid-thirties. She vaguely recognised him from the town. The German soldiers called up to him. Reluctantly he made his way down to the house. One of the Germans barked at him in Polish.

'Well?'

The man took his cap off and held it tightly in his hands, screwing it around, as if it were a wet dishcloth. He glanced at the mute in the doorway and then away, settling his gaze on the soldier's polished boots.

'There were some of them in the woods,' the Pole stammered. He nodded in the direction of the woods on the other side of the road at the top of the farm. 'Last night, the night before. They've been around local houses demanding food.'

The soldier turned to the mute.

'What have you seen?' His tone was impatient. He scarcely glanced at Aleksei's dishevelled face, his eyes casting around instead, flicking from window to doorway, to the woods, the well. The other soldiers stood around, following the conversation. Two had moved down to the well. One kicked at a stalk of hay absent-mindedly.

'Answer!' the German shouted.

The mute stood back a pace. His shoulders rose and his eyes darted about frantically. She saw them sweep across to the hencoop, linger a moment and then move away.

The German stepped forward and punched the mute hard in the stomach. He doubled up and fell with a grunt to the ground.

'Do you know I could have you shot for refusing to answer?' the German barked. 'Do you know what the price is for sheltering vermin?'

The Pole tried to speak, he held up his hand lamely, but the German turned on him viciously, snapping the clip from the leather holster at his waist, from which he half drew a pistol.

'The Poles are no better,' one of the soldiers at the well muttered. 'It's like rats sheltering fleas.'

The other soldier laughed softly. In the hencoop Yael's pulse raced. The German was more or less understandable, similar to her native Yiddish.

The German interrogator turned to the two by the well. 'Search the house,' he yelled. 'See what you find.'

'He's a crazy one,' the Pole finally stuttered, nodding at the mute. 'He don't speak, never has.'

The German cocked his head to one side and gazed at the figure on the floor. The mute's long hair hung over his eyes. He was muttering, coughing, choking, the sounds arising like the bubbling of a brook.

'Mentally retarded?' the German said.

'He's not dangerous, or nothing,' the Pole interjected quickly, his voice shaking with nerves. 'It's just that he don't never seem to have learned to speak.'

'Speech,' the German said, taking a clean handkerchief from his pocket and blowing his nose with it. 'Speech is what makes us human. It is what defines us. It is what civilises us. Without speech we are what? We are no better than beasts, no more significant than dogs, than pigs.'

'Well I don't know about that,' the Pole said. He was shaking his head and realised the German was humouring him. Despite the cold, a line of sweat glistened on his forehead.

The mute had got to his feet. He was taller, and much broader than the German. He brushed his hair back from his face and attempted to tidy his clothes. From behind him the two soldiers pushed out of the house.

'There's nothing in there,' they said, 'just a whole pile of books.'

'Books?' the interrogator laughed. 'What would this dog want with books?' He fingered the pistol in its holster and seemed to be considering. 'We should take him in,' he said. 'It's not right to leave him here, he's no more than an animal.'

'Leave him be,' another of the soldiers remonstrated, 'we've got enough on looking for these partisans.'

The interrogator shook his head, as though

it was against his better judgement. 'You wouldn't leave a stray dog, would you, to starve to death? It's better to kill it. Put it out of its misery.' A thought seemed to strike him. 'And what if he breeds? What then? We would end up with a whole race of them! Mute!'

The other soldiers laughed. 'I could see the benefit of it,' the joker said, nodding his head in the direction of the Pole. 'Anyway, don't worry, the only thing he's going to be having sex with out here is one of the pigs.'

As they turned to leave the mute reached out and touched the arm of the interrogator. The German jumped back and wiped his sleeve as if disgusted. The mute pointed towards the hencoop, a strangulated noise tearing his throat. Yael froze. The mute moved quickly down the path towards the small wooden building. Yael shuffled to the far corner, pushing her back tight against the boards. Her heart was thumping, and yet the blood seemed to have drained from her face. By the house the group of German soldiers looked on bemused. The mute paused a moment by the small door of the hencoop. He glanced back over his shoulder. Opening the door his arm snaked inside. Yael whimpered. The hand reached up, feeling along the shelf, between the sitting hens and quickly, expertly, extracted a number of fresh eggs.

Yael did not see the mute as he made his way back up to the farmyard, his arms full of the eggs. She heard though the sound of the laughter, of their receding feet. The cough of an engine and then silence.

The air hissed from Yael's lungs as she exhaled. She pressed her forehead against the boards. For some moments she struggled to take control of her breathing. Her vision blurred and she thought she was going to faint. Slowly her pulse settled and she leaned back against the side of the coop, her eyes closed.

★　★　★

Later when she looked out, it had started to snow. Thick flakes that fell heavily and rested on the grass like down, not melting, so that a few minutes later they had begun to join up, forming small white islands, spreading, colonising the back field. A thin column of smoke rose from the chimneystack of the farmhouse. The mute appeared in the window, his face black against the darkness. He disappeared but a few moments later the door opened.

The footprints he left in the snow were large. He stopped at the hencoop and opened the flap. His face appeared in the opening. He beckoned her gently. Without saying a word she followed him up to the house, lingering for a moment on the threshold. He took her arm and gently pulled her in, closing the door behind her.

8

A breeze picked up, blowing the snowflakes against the window of the kitchen. The temperature had dropped so the flakes were crisp and heavy and tapped against the glass. Yael sat on the stool the mute offered her, by the large wooden table. She watched him as he stalked about the kitchen. His movements were slow and deliberate. Often he went to the window and gazed out, or opened the door and stood watching, listening.

He did not seem to know how to behave with Yael. On the one hand he clearly did not want her there and seemed more comfortable in ignoring her presence. On the other hand he seemed bound by some innate sense of good manners that forced him to share with her the basic dinner he prepared for himself and a cup of strong Russian tea.

The mute, it seemed, did not own two cups. For some few minutes he was confounded by this and stood between the tiled stove on which the water was slowly boiling in an open pan and the table on which he had placed the cup and a paper bag filled with loose tea. Yael, seeing his discomfort, shook her head and indicated he should not think about her. Finally however he found a small soup bowl, which he reserved for himself.

He pushed the tea, which he had sweetened with sugar, across to her with a slice of bread. He took his own bowl and sat on a stool by the stove on which he balanced his tea and sandwich. He picked up a book and buried himself in it, and only then, when he seemed able to ignore her presence did he seem able to relax a little. His shoulders dropped and the tight furrows creasing his forehead smoothed out.

Yael drank the tea slowly, each sip an unimaginable pleasure, the warm sweetness scalding her throat. After the meagre meal she felt replete and almost dizzy. When she rose from the table, the mute blinked and his neck stiffened. He bent his face to the pages of the book, which were barely visible in the faint light seeping through the window and lost himself once more in the words.

In the corner of the room she found a coat hanging on a peg. Taking it down she wrapped it around herself. It was a warm winter coat, shabby with age, but thick, fleece-lined and soft. The coat enveloped her. As she drew the collar up around the sides of her face she smelled his musky, earthy scent.

The mute's kitchen was small and sparsely furnished. The main feature of the room was the large table. In the corner of the room was a tiled stove, darkened by years of smoke. Its top surface was not large, but the chimney was thick, and the oven door, which hung open a fraction, was bright with flames that danced inside. On a shelf were jars and paper bags and in the corner a sack filled with potatoes. The floor was wooden; old boards that buckled and creaked under the foot.

Yael curled herself up by the side of the sack of potatoes, out of the draught that came from under the bottom of the door and close enough to the stove to catch a little of its heat without disturbing him. With her stomach warmed by the tea and her body cosseted by the soft warmth of the coat, she drifted to sleep. She woke briefly and was a little disorientated. The mute sat by the stove, still reading, his bare feet propped up on its surface.

An intense feeling of peace settled upon her. I am safe, she thought. For this moment. For this one moment I am safe. And it was enough for her. She fell asleep once more, heavily, deeply, dreamlessly.

9

The mute kept his distance from Yael, as if he was afraid of her. He left her food on the kitchen table and occasionally brewed up strong sweet cups of tea, but beyond that, he seemed unwilling to acknowledge her existence. He spent his time outside, preparing the house and the sty at the bottom of the field where he kept a couple of pigs for the winter, splitting the last of the logs and storing them neatly beneath the tarpaulin against the side of the house. When he came in, he would open the door of the stove, build up the fire and sit by it, lost in one of his books.

When he had gone out one morning, Yael picked up the book he had been reading. It was a volume of Pushkin. One wall of the other room in the house was lined with crudely constructed shelves, tight with books. Russians mainly: Turgenev, Tolstoy, Pushkin, Lermontov and more recent volumes of Gumilyov and Akhmatova. There were translations of French poets and novelists in Russian and Polish along with Shakespeare and Byron.

Yael ran her finger along the dusty books,

feeling the ribbing of the ornate spines, the gloss of the embossed lettering, the rough texture of the cloth on cheaper bound editions and the brittle smoothness of some newer paper-backed books. Her father had only a small number of books in the family home, but she recalled a visit to her grandfather's home in Lomza; a three-storey building with a small cobbled yard. Her mother's father had been pious and his shelves were heavy with books. Copies of the works of the Gaon, Holy books, books by Tsadiks; the Hebrew curious and exotic to Yael's untutored eye. Sitting on the arm of a battered sofa, gazing across the shelves of books, Yael's mind wandered back to the evenings of her childhood in her grandparents' home. Wondering over her grandmother's wigs, her grandfather's shawls. The books in the library, leather-bound, polished with use, almost golden in the light of the *kurnik*, the small lamp stood on his table. In the early evenings small study groups met in his library, pouring over the Talmud, the Mishnah or the Chayei Adam.

She picked an ornate volume from among the books and opened it. Her eyes flicked down across the Cyrillic script, picking out words, her lips mouthing the beginnings of lines. She had studied Russian at school, and had listened often as Josef read aloud from his bed, but she still stumbled, unsure, not fully confident. *Goodbye, my friend*, she read, *Goodbye, my dear one, you are in my breast.*

The door opened and she heard the whisper of wind, the unsettling stillness of a snowstorm, a foot on the floorboards and the sound of the mute blowing against his fingers. The domesticity of it snagged her heart. She thought of her father, her mother, their home. A dry spasm tightened her throat and she felt her eyes burn. '*My neshomeleh*!' her father would call as he entered the house.

When the mute came through the doorway she was crying. The book fell and landed with a thump on the bare boards. She covered her face with her hands and sobbed into them. Sobbed for the life that had gone. For her mother and father, for their home, for the wakening in the night and hearing the sound of her brother's breathing, for the waking in the morning to hear her father humming a song, the swish of her mother's brush on the stone flags of the threshold. For their scolding, for their love, for her doll which she had not long stopped playing with but which sat still beside her pillow. For the rhythm of life and its worn, familiar contours. For her life.

'Oh God, oh God,' she whispered, 'Where have you gone?'

The mute bent by her feet and took up the volume of Yesenin's poems. Closing it carefully, smoothing down the page that had creased, pressing it tight. He did not look at her. His movements were stiff and uncomfortable. Slowly he rose, and slotted the book back onto the shelf, lining it carefully, so that it did not stick out, nor stand indented more than its neighbours. For a moment he lingered, his finger on the spine of the book, and then he turned and walked slowly from the room.

Later Yael went through into the kitchen. Her eyes were sore and the skin of her cheeks felt tight from the tears that had dried on them. The mute was seated at the stove with his back to her, his head bent low over the poems of Pushkin, his feet, shoeless, on the tiled stove once again. She stood by the window and looked out. He turned and seemed about to move, but then shook his head and turned back to the book, allowing her to stay there.

It was snowing hard. The wind drove the heavy flakes against the window and already the ledge had been lost beneath a three-inch ribbon of it. The field was white and the hencoop indistinct. The trees were still dark.

They danced erratically in the wind.

'Thank you,' she whispered, turning to face him.

She saw his head move, but he did not turn. It was little more than a twitch acknowledging she had spoken, then he bent low, his eyes fixed hard upon the lines of text, fiercely losing himself in Pushkin's gypsies.

Yael turned from the window and leaning back against the frame of some cupboarding, regarded him. He was a large man, his skin dark, but smooth, closely, carefully shaven. His clothes were old and patched, but clean. The fingers, which rested upon the edge of the page, ready to turn, were blunt with short cut nails.

'I said 'thank you',' Yael said, a little louder, slightly irritated by his refusal to recognise her.

The mute flinched a little. For a few minutes longer he attempted to read, but then closed the book sharply and placed it on the table. Without looking at her he pushed his feet into his boots and laced them quickly. Rising from his chair, he went to fetch his coat from a peg close to the door. She reached out to touch his arm as he passed.

'My name is Yael,' she tried.

He shied away from her. Slipping his arms into the sleeves, he opened the door, fighting to hold the coat closed as a gust of icy wind blew in, sweeping snow across the wooden floorboards. The door closed sharply behind him. Yael watched through the window as he buttoned up the coat, pulling it tight to him. He stepped out into the snow, which already rose higher than the thick soles of his boots, and made his way down to the well. Drawing up the bucket he unhooked it and carried it back to the house.

In the corner of the kitchen was a large tin tub. Pushing through the door the mute placed the bucket on the floor and hauled the tub onto the top of the tiled stove. He poured the freezing water into it and went out, back into the snow. He repeated this journey a number of times, each time returning with a thicker layer of snow on his jacket, freezing in his hair, his bare hands scarlet, then blue and white. Yael sat on her stool and watched him. He was uncomfortable under her gaze, and hurried his task, slopping water onto the floor. Yael took a rag and wiped it dry. He glanced at her and for the briefest of moments their eyes met. She was not sure whether the look in his eyes was anger or fear.

When at last it seemed he had enough, he secured the latch on the door, pulled off his coat and sat watching as the water slowly warmed, occasionally placing small logs through the cast-iron door into the furnace.

The light had begun to fade when he thrust his hand into the water and seemed to think it warm enough. He laboured it down onto the floor, and lit a candle on the table. He searched around for a while and found at last a small wooden box which he placed carefully on the table. Disappearing into the other room, he came back with a rough cotton towel, faded in its pattern, but clean. He placed it on the table beside the wooden box, which was decorated with a delicate carving of a flower, painted once red and gold, though the paint had mainly flaked away now. At last he seemed content.

He glanced quickly at Yael, who had been watching his careful work with some bemusement. He indicated the water and the towel and box with a sharp, nervous waft of his hand. With that he walked from the kitchen and drew a thin curtain over the door, giving her privacy.

10

For some moments Yael was rooted to her stool, confounded at his kindness. She stood up nervously and went to kneel by the tin tub. The water was deep enough to cover half her thigh and the tub wide enough for her to sit in. Lifting the cuff of her shirt, she tested the temperature. Steam rose from the surface. Stepping back across to the doorway, she delicately lifted the edge of the curtain. The mute had lit a candle and was seated by the far window, a book in his hands, engrossed once more.

She stripped slowly and carefully, peeling the clothes from her body. Lice dropped onto the floor and scuttled across the bare floorboards, fat, gorged with blood. Her body was etched with numerous strings of bites, where they had moved across her, the scabs picked at, bloody and sore. Her feet were blistered and sores and bruises peppered her legs. The months of hard living showing on her skin.

She placed her clothes across the stool. The water she stepped into was hot, but bearable. She lowered herself into it and felt the heat rush through her. The steam rose and moistened her face. Droplets soon condensed on her skin, on the split tips of her lank hair, on the pink, delicate skin of her nipples. She cupped the water in her hands and poured it over her, rinsed her face, felt the delight of the hot water running in rivulets down her back. The wooden box contained an old bar of fragrant soap, dry and hard. She dropped it into the water and let it moisten a little.

When she had scrubbed herself so hard her mottled skin turned pink and looked for a moment almost healthy, she stood up. The itching remained. Stepping from the water, she tiptoed across the boards, leaving a trail of water on the floor. She found what she wanted by the side of a small mirror. Taking the mirror and the razor back across to the tub, she carefully shaved the fine pale hairs from her body; the disgust she felt at handling the flat-bodied lice that clung to her was considerably less than her desire to be clean of them.

When the water had grown cooler, she got out. Taking the bucket of cold water stood by the door, she heated it up, feeding more wood into the stove, until the heat was so intense she was forced to close the door. With the hot water she washed her hair over the tub, scrubbing it hard, so that the water, when she had finished, was dark with the dirt. Then carefully she dried herself. She found a comb on the shelf and combed through her hair ferociously, taking handfuls of it out in the process. Cleaning the comb and the shaving knife as best as she could, she dropped them into the pot of bubbling water on the stove and let them simmer there.

She could not bear the idea of putting on her old clothes, so she wrapped the damp towel around her and slipped the mute's coat over the top. Opening the door of the stove, she carefully poked in her clothes. Her underwear first, which popped and crackled as the lice exploded, then her blouse and finally her skirt which dampened the flames and sent up an acrid, foul-smelling smoke that hung in a fug beneath the ceiling.

She found an old curtain folded on a shelf. The material was coarse cotton, faded by years of sunlight. She found a needle and thread and she sat sewing a skirt, taking enormous pleasure in this task, carefully drawing up a pattern, making sure the seam was neat. She heard the mute's footsteps and then his nervous cough as he stood behind the curtain. Trying the skirt on, together with one of his shirts, she stood and admired the effect in the small mirror, having to hold it at many different angles to see herself properly.

'I'm decent,' she called, realising only as he hesitantly poked his head through the cloth that she had used Yiddish, as if he were her brother.

'Almost human again,' she said.

★ ★ ★

The mute had seemed oblivious to the change in her appearance. Whenever it was possible he avoided her, working for hours outside in the freezing conditions, coming in, covered in snow, hands blue with cold. If she attempted to care for him at these times he reacted angrily, brushing past her stiffly, eyes averted, as if she did not exist. When inside he would busy himself with some chore, or take up a book. Only occasionally would she glance up and find he had been watching her, before he quickly looked away.

When one evening she caught his eye, as she was at the table drinking a cup of scalding sweet tea, she smiled. His face flushed with embarrassment and he stood up sharply, knocking over his chair with a clatter. Picking it up, he stumbled. He pushed his feet into his boots and grabbed his coat from the peg. The door slammed back against the wall and a flurry of snow skittered across the kitchen as he plunged out into the darkness.

'Aleksei,' she called from the doorway as the wind whipped at her clothes and snapped her hair back from her face. 'Aleksei . . .'

Yael huddled in the corner of the kitchen she had made her own, the flame of the candle dancing in the wind that found the gaps around the door and window. 'Aleksei,' she whispered, trying the name on her tongue, finding that with the use of it he became more real, a person, somebody whose presence she desired back in the kitchen. 'Yael,' she whispered too, and wondered how long it had been since she had heard her own name spoken. How long in fact it had been since she had properly spoken to somebody. Not since Rivka's death and that had been in the autumn, when it had still been warm enough to sleep in the woods.

If nobody knows I am here, she thought, if there is nobody to say my name, then do I really exist? But the mute knows I exist, she thought, Aleksei knows I am here, that I'm alive.

At intervals during the night she went over to the door, and opening it carefully, called out into the darkness. The wind whipped away her voice so she was barely able to hear it herself. The light from the candle immediately went out, sizzling in the sticky, liquid wax. Yael curled herself into a small

60

ball beneath Aleksei's coat and finally slept.

She dreamt of her father, on the doorstep of their home, tacks sticking from between his lips. 'It's in stillness God is found,' he said. But the tacks became black teeth and instead of her father she found she was sitting with a lunatic who had passed through the town when she was a small child, his beard reaching almost to his waist, his hair as white as icicles. '*Ódem yeséyde mey-ófer v'séyfe l'ófer!*' He whispered as though this wisdom was a secret, to be shared covertly. '*Béyne-l'véyne iz óber gut a trunk bromfin!*' And with that he laughed, loudly, rudely, slapping his knees. *Man is from dust and will return to dust. In the meantime it's good to have a sip of vodka!* 'He's not wrong,' she recalled her father saying, when she had awoken and lay breathing heavily, sweat dampening her brow.

11

Aleksei did not return that night, nor in the morning. Yael woke late, her head aching. Overnight the storm had blown itself out and half the world had disappeared. The snow lay deep across the back field, banking in a soft white rise to the wall of the house, nearly lipping the windowsill. The clouds had dispersed and with the clear sky, the temperature had begun to drop and Yael could hear the house creak as the wood contracted.

Wrapping herself up warm, she struggled out, a wave of snow tumbling onto the floorboards as she opened the door. She was breathless as she waded through the stiffening crust of snow and dug out some wood from the pile beneath the tarpaulin. The cold air scolded her cheeks and her chin. Her fingers froze to the chopped logs. With an armful she hurried back, pushing the door closed with difficulty.

Later, when the wood was burning in the stove and the room had heated up, Yael stood by the window and gazed out into the whiteness through the narrow circles that were now opaque with frost and snow. There was no way he would survive out in the open. Where had he gone? She paced back and forth, brewed a cup of tea, leaving enough hot water in the pan, in case he should at that moment push back through the door. But he did not.

The light began to fail soon after midday. The snow was washed with a pink hue, the delicacy of which belied the lethal nature of the cold. The bellies of the undulations were blue.

Yael wandered through the two rooms of the small house, traced her fingers along the spines of his books, gazed at the print on the wall, a mediocre painting of a river running through a forest at sunset, the garish colours fading gently with age. Yael imagined the time in the far future when the scene would finally be engulfed by night. At the end of one of the bookshelves was a large leather-bound volume, uninscribed. Yael eased it out and opened it. Beneath a sheet of thin tissue paper a face peered. It was an album of photographs. Seating herself in Aleksei's seat, she carefully turned back the protective page and examined the photograph of a middle-aged man, beard still dark though flecked with grey. He was well-dressed, his collar new and pinned tightly at his throat, in his left hand a cane, the bone handle cradled loosely in his palm. The photographer's name was at the bottom of the print, and the address of his studio in St Petersburg.

Over the following pages were various family photographs. The middle-aged man grew old and then, as she turned the page, died. In his coffin he lay stiff, his face sunken, nose turned beak-like in death. Around him his family gazed into the photographer's lens, seemingly obliviously to his corpse. Only one woman ignored the photographer, a young woman who gazed down, her face a mask of sorrow, her lips pressed tight, one against the other, her hand reaching out slightly, seemingly instinctively to touch the folded hand of the dead man. By her side stood a small child, barely visible. His head was pressed close against the woman's thigh. His eyes were wide, and his lower lip drooped, as if he was struck by awe.

Yael eased the corners of the photograph carefully from their holders and lifted it away from the page. Turning it over she found on its reverse ornate Russian script. *Father's funeral*, it read, *December 23rd 1912*. She turned it over again and examined the young woman. The grief-stricken daughter had long dark hair, coiled beneath a loose black lace headscarf. Her features were fine, her large, almond-shaped eyes beautiful and exotic. She was vaguely familiar. The little boy, no more than two or three years old, was undoubtedly her son. He shared her dark hair and eyes. The same exotic beauty. It was Aleksei. The mute.

Yael examined the photograph carefully. She carried the album across to the bed, which stood closer to the window where it was lighter. This photograph had also been taken in Russia, as had the next, which was of the same woman and child. With the two of them, though stood slightly apart, was a man in his early twenties. The style of his clothing seemed slightly old-fashioned and he held a cane. It was not that he distanced himself from his wife and his child, Yael thought, scrutinising the family group, her eyes flicking from one of the figures to another, it was more that the man seemed self-sufficient, while the woman seemed to withdraw. The young boy clung to her, his small hand clutching her skirt, his head inclining towards her, while still he gazed at the photographer with the same awe-struck expression, loose-lipped, eyes wide.

The following pages were peopled by blunt faces of the provincial middle class, one group of distinguished men, in formal dress, at the back of which, with barely his head showing, was Aleksei's father. Yael turned over quickly, three more stiff pages, the tissue paper crackling before she found them again.

1917. Augustow. Poland. Aleksei would have been about five. Dark shadows beneath his mother's eyes. His father still stood apart, his suit a little looser, his collar worn. He leaned against the stick, one hand clasped on top of the other and stared into the camera, seemingly unaware of his wife and son.

The next photograph did not have a date. The photographer's studio address was written neatly in gold lettering across the bottom though. It was on Warsaw Street in Selo. The same one she had herself visited on a number of occasions with her parents and Josef. Aleksei was a couple of years older. His pretty, open face gazed steadily, seriously into the camera, while he leaned in against the side of his mother. The young woman's face was thinner, the skin still darker beneath her beautiful eyes. She was stunning, Yael thought, touching the surface of the photograph softly. There was something tragic about her. Her husband was not in the photograph.

Yael turned over the page, but there were no more photographs. She flicked through the rest of the album but it was empty.

The light had almost gone. Yael stood up. There was a lamp on the small bedside table; she lit it and pulled down the glass. As she lifted the album to put it back on the shelf, a photograph fell and landed at her feet. She bent down and picked it up, taking it over to the bed. She sat down beside the lamp.

She recognised the graveyard, it was in Selo. The coffin was sealed. He stood by the grave, his body rigid, staring bleakly ahead at the lens of the camera. Around him were a few people. His father, leaning heavily on a walking stick, gazing away across the low headstone as though this funeral had nothing to do with him. An Orthodox priest who looked uncomfortable and haughty. Two young men, gravediggers, stood at a distance. Yael's gaze returned to Aleksei. The petrified grimace tore her heart. His arms hung stiff and straight by his sides as if he was stood to attention. No one reached out to touch him. No hand rested upon his shoulder. No body was there for him to lean against. He stood alone, his eyes wide with fear.

In the kitchen she heard the sound of the door handle. Her heart turned. She stood up, the photograph clasped tightly in her hand. The door opened and then closed. She found her legs were trembling and she sat back down on the edge of the bed. There was a moment's silence, before she heard the rustle of a coat falling to the floor and footsteps crossing the kitchen.

12

Aleksei stood in the doorway and wordlessly she looked up at him, the photograph clasped still in her hand.

'I'm sorry,' she whispered.

He stepped over and took the photograph. He did not look angry. He stood for a moment before her and then he turned and placed it in the album on the shelf.

*   *   *

Yael was careful over the next few days. She kept out of his way, busying herself quietly. If she looked up and found he had been watching her once again, she averted her eyes and did not make it obvious she had noticed. The tension of the first few days began to ease and the mute did not disappear again. Silently they shared their meals at the old wooden kitchen table, as if they ate alone. When Aleksei boiled water on the tiled stove, he made strong sweet tea for Yael too, leaving it on the table, rather than giving it to her; and she would make no fuss about drinking it.

The week before Christmas the temperature continued to fall. On Christmas Day it was so cold branches began to break from trees and it was difficult to keep the water in the well from freezing. Instead they began to rely on the snow which they would collect in buckets and leave to melt by the side of the stove.

The more Yael struggled to make herself unobtrusive in the house, to avoid confronting his glance, the more she became sensitive to his presence. There was not a moment when she did not know where he was or what he was doing. As his nervousness of her lessened she felt him observe her more closely, more openly. Despite the longing for contact, she affected ignorance of his gaze. She became so sensitive to it, she knew without looking up if his eyes had slid from the book before him and crept over to her. She felt it like fingers on her back, stroking her, caressing her.

She became more careful of her appearance and noticed, glancing in the small mirror one morning, the colour had risen in her cheeks. She would not call attention to herself, but would long for that quiet, still moment in the day, as she sat sewing, her head bent over the cloth, and he was lounged with his feet on the stove, Lermontov on his lap, when she would notice the difference in the pattern of his breathing, the minute, barely perceptible lowering of its pitch. All at once her skin prickled, as though suddenly coming to life. Her heart quickened and she became for that moment more alive to the texture of the cloth, to the sharpness of the needle, to the exact quality of the light, to the blood that pumped through the veins in her fingers, in her slim wrists.

One evening while bathing in the tin tub in front of the tiled stove, she noticed she had forgotten to pull closed the curtain between the two rooms. Aleksei was reading in the other room and could not see her, but in the silence she became acutely aware of him. She was kneeling in the water which barely covered her thighs. Lifting a jug from the floorboards she filled it, conscious that through the doorway he could hear the burble of water, the slop and creak of the bath as she moved, each drip that fell from her body. Closing her eyes she tilted back her head and poured the water over her face, luxuriating in the way it flowed down across her body, separating around her breasts, circling her naval. When she had finished, she pulled a cotton sheet around her loosely and stood by the open door, allowing the water to drip from her, her flesh more vividly alive, more sensitive to the run of a droplet of water, to the breath of wind, to the softness of the air than ever she had felt it before. Goosebumps dimpled her pale flesh. A deep ache awoke inside her, so suddenly painful she almost groaned.

When, in the mornings, Aleksei shaved, Yael would settle herself at the kitchen table with a book and pretend to be engrossed. Covertly she would watch over the top of the page the quiet slow ritual. He would arrange along the top of the stove, in a neat line, the knife with which he shaved, an old brush, the hairs of which had become soft with age, the bar of soap in its ornamental wooden box, the lid of which he would remove and place alongside, and a metal bowl. Once the water had begun to bubble in the pan on the stove, he poured half carefully into the bowl, lathered his brush and applied the soap to his face. She enjoyed the smooth dexterity of his movements, the ripple of tendons on his bare back, the way he would flick the dark curls of his hair from his face.

On the wall close to the door, beside the hooks on which he hung his coats, a calendar was pinned. It was a cheap wall calendar, illustrated with no pictures. One morning Yael stood by it, gazing up at the dates. She heard his footstep on the floorboards behind her

72

and, thinking he had come to take his coat, moved quietly aside. He did not brush past her, however, nor reach out for his fleece-lined jacket. Instead he stopped a step behind her, so close she could feel his breath on the bare skin of the back of her neck. Yael stiffened. A flush of blood coloured her cheeks. For a few moments he stood silently behind her, then raised his arm, over her shoulder and placed his fingertip on the calendar. So confused was Yael by his proximity, by the intimacy of this movement, she did not at first notice the date on which his nail rested. It was only when he lifted it slightly and tapped the card that she saw it was the thirty-first of December. That it was New Year's Eve. The last day of 1941.

Yael turned, slowly. He did not move. His eyes flicked away from her, settling anxiously on the calendar. The air seemed sharp suddenly, as if charged with electricity.

'It's New Year's Eve,' she whispered, her voice, so unused to speaking, no more than a breath. Aleksei's hand fell back to his side. His head bent away from her but he did not move. She repeated the phrase softly, this time in Russian, enunciating each word with clear schoolgirl care. Slowly he nodded. They stood so close she could reach out and touch him. She could lift up her hand and stroke the line of his jaw, the pink lobe of his ear which showed beneath his hair, the vein that ran down his neck.

The floorboards sighed. A crow called from close to the door. The day was silent. He breathed, she breathed. The blood pulsed in her veins. The muscle in the lid of his eye flickered. It hurt when she swallowed and she wondered if he had heard the dry gulp. He turned then and crossed the kitchen and sat on his stool by the stove. He did not touch the book. She moved to the table and gripped its surface to support her. Her cheeks burned. She could not look at him. Stiffly she set about clearing the cup and plates from the table. She knelt by the wooden bucket in which they washed their dishes and rinsed them carefully. She heard him get up and walk through to the other room. For ten minutes she knelt on the wooden floor, the plates shimmering beneath the water and struggled to regain control of her breathing.

For the rest of the day they moved about the house silently, occupied with the tasks that needed doing: the boiling of porridge for the pigs, feeding the fowl, bringing in fresh wood and keeping the stove alive. When they entered the same room, they avoided looking at each other. Yael found her hands shook slightly. She wondered if he had planned on celebrating the New Year, as often her neighbours had done in Selo, but as the light faded and the kitchen dissolved into darkness, he opened the door, as was often his custom, and smoked a cigarette. When he had stubbed it out, he came back inside and ate the normal thin broth and drank a cup of tea and wandered through into his room.

Yael heard the springs of his bed creak. The house was so silent she could hear the pulse of blood in her ears, her unsteady breathing. Though it had grown dark Yael felt no desire to sleep. It was hard to make out the contours of the kitchen furniture, the only thing visible was the bright outline of the door of the stove. She felt oddly unsettled, her limbs prickled with desire for something.

To occupy herself, she tried to recreate in her mind her family home; each corner, each surface, each picture on the wall. The face of her mother, of her father, of Josef. But despite her efforts, the walls shimmered indistinctly, the faces disintegrated, crumbling away as quickly as she built them. Perversely she found the face of her grandfather rose clearly and unbidden, his features so distinct, she felt she could reach and touch them.

As a small child Yael had never felt comfortable with her grandfather, had been even a little frightened of him. She had never relished the family's visits to Lomza. Partly this was because of the old man's obvious and bluntly spoken disapproval of his son-in-law. Her father had been a student as a young man in one of her grandfather's Talmud classes and it had been before these classes he had met Reb Silverstein's daughter. Her father had wanted to move to Warsaw and study. Already as a young man, he had begun to talk romantically about Palestine, a source of conflict with his future father-in-law. Selo had been the poor compromise.

In the darkness of Aleksei's kitchen her grandfather's face hovered before Yael. The leather strap of the phylactery, bound so tight the veins protruded on his arms. The box on his forehead. The shawl, thinning with age. The way his body bobbed from the waist, backward and forward, in short pecking motions as he prayed. The way his eyes shone as he told them stories in the light of the *kurnik*.

Each story was laced with bitterness: 'Like the Passover meal,' he whispered passionately. 'Our lives are seasoned with bitter herbs. As it says in the book of Ruth, *Call me Mara, because the Almighty has made my life very bitter!*'

As she lay down upon her bed in the corner of the room, the story of Ruth drifted through her mind. For some time she lay on her back, covered by Aleksei's coat, the tale spinning in the darkness. Her heart lurched. She sat up. She paused and listened. Heart thumping, she stepped noiselessly across the floorboards.

A pale moon illuminated his room. He had not drawn the curtains and the light lay slick and ghostly across the sheets of his bed. She paused a moment inside the door, her heart thumping so hard she thought she would turn back. He did not stir. She could not hear his breathing. He did not move when she lifted the corner of his blanket at the foot of the bed and lay down. At first she hardly dare move. The air was cold. She drew herself up into a tight ball, easing herself backwards, until the blanket covered her and she was able to wrap it beneath her. She felt his foot pressed against the small of her back. Her body stiffened, but he did not shift. He did not rise. Slowly she relaxed. The warmth of his bed crept into her muscles. She slept.

★   ★   ★

The next morning when Aleksei turned from the doorway, tossing out the stub of his cigarette, his head ducked nervously seeing that she was watching him. Quickly Yael bent over the stove setting the water to boil for tea. At the table they avoided looking into each other's eyes.

13

The brutal cold lasted into the New Year. The temperature continued to drop until, as Yael read on an old thermometer attached to the wall, it hit minus thirty. In the week that followed it was difficult to go out, and Aleksei only left the house to feed the pigs. The chickens he moved into the pigsty, to benefit from the warmth of the close proximity of the pigs.

The world seemed to retreat. Venturing out one evening, as the sun was setting, Yael stood for some minutes at the edge of the wood. The snow reached up to her thigh. The trees were black against the intense purity of the untrodden expanse of whiteness. Not one sound was audible; no bird, no animal, no voice, no engine, no breath or stir of wind. Yael had never experienced a silence more crushing.

Aleksei had an old radio, more primitive even than the one her father had listened to each Saturday afternoon. Occasionally Yael would turn it on and wait while it hummed and whistled and warmed up. Carefully she would twist the large dial, searching through the static haze for the whisper of a voice, which proved they were not the only ones alive.

The German invasion had been slowed to almost a halt by the fierceness of the winter. Their tanks, unsuited to the poor roads and the bitter cold, made slow progress. Soldiers were dying of hypothermia and disease. Hitler had ordered that they stand firm. The Soviet army, meanwhile, more accustomed to the conditions, had launched a counter attack, advancing in some places as much as a hundred miles. Yael thought of Josef.

Aleksei did not listen to the radio. It did not seem to concern him when Yael turned it on, but he would invariably walk through into the kitchen and tend to the stove, or lose himself in one of his books. Occasionally, when Yael picked up a station that was playing music, he would shuffle in. His dark eyes fixed upon the radio apparatus and he would be lost in the flow of strings, the rise and fall of the melody, the drama.

One evening, as he pushed logs into the stove and gazed distractedly at the fierce dance of the flames, Yael picked up the book he had been reading. It was a collection of poems by Akhmatova, her profile etched on the front. Yael read out the first line of the poem from the page the book was open on.

Song of the Last Meeting. Her voice sounded odd at first and she coughed and cleared her throat and began again. Aleksei glanced up from the flames. For a moment their eyes met, before she focused once more upon the lines. She noticed he continued to watch her.

'*Amid the maples an autumn whisper pleaded: 'Die with me!'*'

Her voice trembled, no more than a hoarse whisper, yet clear, distinct, in the evening's silence. When she paused at the end of the poem and looked up, she found that Aleksei was still watching her. His eyes glistened.

'Did you like that?' she whispered.

He nodded slowly.

As the evening hours melted slowly with the wax of the candles, Yael read to him, poem after poem from the Akhmatova collection, her voice growing more confident, more expressive, whilst also remaining soft, little more than a whisper. Later they lay on the bed and she read once more from the *Song of the Last Meeting.* 'This is the song of the final meeting/I glanced at the house's dark frame. / Only the bedroom candles burning / with an indifferent yellow flame.'

Aleksei's eyes were closed. She shut the book and allowed it to fall onto the sheets. The candle extinguished at that moment, throwing the room into darkness. When she turned she could barely see the outline of his face.

'Are you sleeping?'

His eyes opened and he turned, hitching himself up, resting on his elbow. They were barely a foot apart. Yael could feel the soft stir of his breath on her face, the back of her arm. She did not speak. She rested her head against his hard pillow and closed her eyes. She listened to his breathing, felt the almost imperceptible movement of the bed with each inhalation and exhalation. They slept like that. Side by side. Woke in the morning to sunlight, her body curled, back to his, touching slightly.

From then on it became their ritual, the reading. Pushkin, Lermontov, Tolstoy, Byron, Shelley, Blok, an old copy of Rilke Yael found pushed away at the back of the shelf, which Aleksei did not seem to understand, but listened to, and Yael struggled with. '*Ich bin auf der Welt zu allein und doch nich allein genug um jede Stunden zu weihen.*'

When he touched her face, her cheek tingled as if he had caressed it with live wires. As they lay in bed she wrapped her arms around him, pushed her forehead between his shoulder blades, the scent of his sleeping body filling her nostrils, the wide warmth of him comforting her. During the daylight hours she could not bear when he was not in the room with her. She followed him from one room to the other, like a dog on the heels of a child. When, as the weather began to improve a little, he made the journey into Selo to trade a pig for some much needed provisions, she retreated to a corner of the house and sat there, fretting, biting her nails, her heart lurching at every sound, longing for him to be back. For the quiet order of their life to be restored.

The first thaw broke her heart. The first blade of grass cut her like a knife. She could not bear the idea winter might end, that she might lose the tight intimacy of their circumscribed routines. As long as the snow bound them in, as long as the freezing temperatures made going outside difficult, she felt this peace might be preserved, that this unreal, tiny world, this dream of how a life could be, might somehow survive.

As each day passed Aleksei allowed a little more of himself to be revealed. The rigidity of his fear began to loosen. Yael found they could look into each other's eyes and he would not shy away. She could reach forward and run her fingers through his hair, and pull him closer, so that her lips touched the rough stubble of his jaw and he would lean in to her. She would smile and find it mirrored in his face. She loved the way it grew, building up slowly on his face, starting in his eyes, the skin tightening, his cheeks dimpling, the line of his upper lip rising, until his whole face was radiant with it.

'You're not crazy,' she murmured in his ear, using the Yiddish word. 'You are not a *meshúgener*. It is the world that is crazy. This crazy world has made you sane.'

Aleksei was gentle with her. His fingers fluttered across her skin. When he looked at her his eyes seemed full of wonder. When she undressed he would turn away, conscious of her embarrassment. Even when she desired him to look at her, to take in the wonder of her young woman's body, he would shyly close his eyes and allow her to take his hand and direct him.

As the days and months passed, the snow receded. The buds fattened on the branches of the birch and oak. Shoots pierced the dark earth. Yael was torn by the irony that with the spring, with this resurrection of the earth, war once more became possible; death could continue its rampage across the continent.

At night Yael curled up against Aleksei, seeking comfort in his proximity. Is it possible, she thought, that here, in the middle of war, as on all sides carnage and murder stalk the world, is it possible that there can exist this pocket of peace? Of joy? Of sanity? Are there more? She pictured then this hideaway replicated across the fields, across the country, across the continent, a string of candles flickering in the darkness, fragile flames. If this is possible, she thought, then there is hope for earth. There is hope.

14

April 3rd was Yael's birthday. In the corner of
the field, in the shade of the old oak, was a
dark hill of ice, it was all that remained of
winter. The trees were alive with spring and
when Yael walked out early, down the field
and stood at the edge of the trees, the sound
of the birds seemed brash and forceful after
the tranquillity of the snow. The leaves curled
from their tight buds, sticky with sap, their
green almost yellow. Delicate. Insistent. The
grass was thickening beneath her heels. She
could feel it almost, the explosive fecundity of
earth, its sharp, dark stink. Life bristling,
thrusting, surging. It frightened her.

Seeing her stood there, as the sun rose and
the thin mist rose from the earth, dissipating
in its soft warmth, Aleksei rushed out down
the path and took her arm and pulled her
back to the house. He shook his head and
from his throat uttered unintelligible syllables
that nonetheless emphasised his fear.

'It's early,' Yael said, 'Nobody will see me.'

But Aleksei shook his head. For the first
time in months Yael saw the look of panic
flicker in his eyes. His fingers shook as they

fingered the cloth of her skirt. She lifted her hand and stroked his face.

'It's fine,' she whispered, comforting him. 'It's all right. I will stay inside. Don't worry.'

Later, she put aside the book she had been reading. Aleksei had been working outside for most of the day, mending fences, repairing the tiles on the roof and she had been bored alone in the house. Aleksei was at the kitchen table sharpening a knife.

'It's my birthday,' she said.

He looked up and fixed his eyes upon her. The knife hung in his hand, reflecting the last ray of sunlight falling through the kitchen window.

'Today,' she said. 'I'm sixteen.'

Aleksei laid the knife on the table, but did not move to get up. He continued to gaze at her. The expression in his eyes, the slight rise of his brows, suggested confusion, rather than joy or interest, as though he was searching somewhere in the back of his mind, attempting to interpret her words into a language he understood. She checked her Russian, tried it again, enunciating it with care. His forehead creased and slowly he shook his head.

'It's all right,' Yael whispered, 'we don't need to celebrate.'

He stood then and stumbled over to her.

Grasping her in his arms he hugged her tight and she laughed. Aleksei's body shook and a moment later Yael realised he was crying. The tears streamed silently down his face.

'What is it?'

He buried his head in the crook of her neck and she felt the warm tears trickling down her skin, tracing a line between her breasts. She ran her fingers through his hair, bewildered.

'What is it, Aleksei?' she whispered, 'What is it?'

But the answer was lost in his silence.

★   ★   ★

One morning, as spring advanced, Aleksei opened the large old wardrobe stood in the corner of his bedroom and emptied it of clothes. Methodically, with utmost care, he laid the shirts and trousers, the one suit and sheets kept there across his bed. From beneath an old blanket he removed a parcel wrapped with brown paper. This he held reverentially. He laid it on the top of the other clothes, with delicacy, skimming his hand across its fading surface, his finger teasing the thin string with which it was tied.

'What are we doing?' Yael asked.

Aleksei pointed not at the clothes but at the back of the deep wardrobe.

'Cleaning?'

Aleksei shook his head. From the work shed he brought tools and a large sheet of wood so thin it buckled as he carried it, reminding Yael of the young man who had sat at the side of the stage, before the war, during Rivka's performance of *The Slaughter* creating atmospheric sound effects with half coconuts and a sheet of metal and a little drum.

At the back of the wardrobe Aleksei created a partition, no more than a foot and a half wide. He hinged it from the inside, so that when he pushed it shut it was impossible to tell that it was not the back, unless you had seen the true depth of it before hand. He indicated for Yael to climb in.

'Inside?' Yael said, uncomprehending. 'Why?'

He insisted, however, taking her arm and pushing her forward. The wardrobe stood about seven feet tall and four feet wide. Two dark wood panels ran across the bottom, between which it was possible to see the floor. She stepped onto these carefully, unsure they would hold her weight. Turning, she looked at Aleksei enquiringly. He pushed gently, until she was stood at the far back of the wardrobe, then pressed the partition closed, squashing her.

'No!' she protested, but Aleksei held tight to the wood, holding it from the other side until she stopped struggling.

The space behind the partition was barely enough for her to stand in. The tightness of it was overwhelming. A thin light shone by her feet, but the space was too narrow for her to adjust her head to look down. Yael felt the pressure grow in her chest. A weight seemed to press down upon it, stopping her from breathing. She gasped. Perspiration prickled her skin. Panic surged through her veins.

When at last Aleksei opened the partition, she stepped out quickly, her face red, and gasped deeply at the fresh air.

'I can't,' she gasped. 'I can't go in there.'

Aleksei merely nodded. She sat on the bed and watched while he carefully repacked the wardrobe, making sure access to the space behind the partition was easy. Yael was angry.

'It's too small,' she complained. 'I couldn't breathe in there.'

The last item he picked up from the bed was the paper package. He lifted it with care and carried it across to the wardrobe, but then turned and hesitated. Slowly he turned and looked at Yael.

'It's true,' she moaned. 'I couldn't go in there again.'

He walked back across to her and lowered

himself onto the bed beside her. The package he placed on her lap.

'What?' she said, 'What is it?'

Aleksei nodded at the package.

'You want me to open it?'

Slowly, seriously, without smiling, he nodded again. The paper and the string were old and dusty. Yael struggled with the knot and was tempted to simply pull the string off and rip open the paper, but the reverence with which he had carried it and placed it on her lap stopped her.

Finally the knot gave and the string unfolded. She turned the package over and opened up the sheet of paper. Inside, neatly folded, were some women's clothes. She looked up at Aleksei, but he was no longer looking at her, his eyes were fixed upon the flowered silk blouse Yael felt between her fingers. She lifted the blouse, allowing it to fall out of its creases.

'It's lovely,' she gasped. The silk felt exquisitely smooth between her fingers. She brought it close and rubbed it gently against her cheek. 'It's beautiful.'

With the blouse were a trim black skirt, a dress and two more blouses. She laid each one out carefully across the bed, revelling in the beautiful material, the fine tailoring. The clothes were obviously expensive and well made. Though they were old, they were well preserved, and, Yael discovered as she held them close to her face, delicately fragrant. She held one up to Aleksei.

'Smell it,' she said.

Aleksei breathed in, nervously. The scent seemed to cut at his nostrils, a muscle twitched in his cheek. He lifted his hand and took the dress and pulled it closer to his face and smelled it again. His face seemed to crumple then. A tear slid down his cheek, settling in the crease of his tight-pursed lip.

'Aleksei,' Yael whispered. 'Are you all right?' And then after a while, 'Were they your mother's?'

For some moments she did not think he was going to answer, but then he nodded and looked up at her. She put her hand on his. His lips twitched and then he smiled, a small, frail smile.

'Oh Aleksei,' she whispered and leant forward and took him in her arms. But he pulled back and indicated the clothes. He pointed at Yael and held up the blouse.

'You want me to try them on?'

★   ★   ★

By late spring Yael had regained most of the weight she had lost during the autumn in the

92

forest. The clothes fitted her neatly, and gazing into the small mirror, having tied back her hair with a ribbon, Yael surprised herself with her own attractiveness. Aleksei gazed at her from the edge of the bed and in his eyes she realised for the first time in her life the power she was able to command over another. The thought did not bring her joy, as she might have imagined; rather her heart squeezed with sympathy for him and she took off the elegant skirt, the fine silk blouse and wrapped them tenderly back in the wrapping paper. Aleksei did not protest. He tied the package and placed it back inside the wardrobe and they did not take it out again.

With the improved weather they fell into a circumscribed routine and Yael, though frustrated that she could not leave the house, except after dark, felt a sense of contentment she could only wonder at.

Was this then love? she wondered. Not a fairy tale, not the romance and passion she had dreamt of. Not dramatic. Not inexplicable. But rather this deep, penetrating thankfulness for the kindness of another. This wakening with the faith that somebody would care for her. Late in the evening she read some Mayakovsky. The simple refrain caught her heart and she whispered it again, before they slept.

'*Beside your love / I have / no ocean . . . Beside your love / I have / no sun.*'

She was not sure why the words seemed so meaningful, except that she could conceive of no other world beyond the confines of those two rooms. Beyond the two of them, no other people.

15

The summer was endless. Long, claustrophobic hot days when the sun rose almost as soon as it set and scorched a slow path across the cloudless sky, lingering late into the evening, losing little of its power. Yael lived for the moment when they would lie down on the bed, the windows open to the night, covered only by a thin cotton sheet. Even then, there was little escape from the oppressive heat and the sheets would be damp with sweat within minutes and Yael would wake from some dream, her whole body prickling torturously.

'I have to go out,' Yael begged. 'I'm going to go mad stuck in these two rooms day after day!'

Aleksei made the trip into town more often and brought back with him books and newspapers and from these she kept track of the fighting. One day he brought the newspaper home and laid it flat upon the table pressing his finger against the text. *Persons found disobeying existing orders against the Jews, by hiding them, maintaining them or helping them by any means are*

95

committing a serious criminal act. Any person found to be disobeying these laws within the district, irrespective of age or sex, will be arrested and detained. If Jews perform acts of sabotage, all residents of the locality where the accused Jews lived, will be held responsible.

The acts of sabotage had become more frequent as the weather improved. A railway line had been blown up just outside Selo and a German unit had been fired upon. Twenty miles to the south, two German soldiers had been killed by a homemade mine. In response, the Germans had taken five men from the village and shot them in the market square as an example.

Late one evening in September, the sun had gone down and a low mist had settled over the field at the back of the house. Aleksei had been out to feed the chickens while Yael had cooked porridge on the stove. They ate less meat since the Germans had issued an order in late August confiscating the last of Aleksei's pigs.

She had just served it into two bowls on the table, when Aleksei came in. He nodded and grinned seeing the steaming bowls. The summer lingered still, with bright cloudless days, the sun too hot to sit in at midday. But in the evenings, it had begun to grow colder and the scent of autumn hung on the damp air.

There was a knock on the kitchen door. Yael and Aleksei froze.

'Hey!' a voice called and the door creaked open.

Yael dashed through to the back room and threw herself onto the floor of the bedroom, knocking the air from her lungs. Gasping, she rolled beneath the bed. She heard heavy footfalls on the kitchen floor. Aleksei's grunt as he was thrown against the table.

'You alone?' the voice demanded in Polish.

'There are two bowls,' another voice said.

'Who else is here?'

With her ear pressed against the floorboards, Yael felt the reverberation of the men's footfalls as they entered the bedroom. For a moment they hesitated. Two boots stood close beside her. They were old and tattered, the sole breaking free of the upper part of the boot. Thick socks were turned down over the ankles. Yael pressed her eyes closed and muttered a silent prayer.

'Va!' a man said. The voice sounded amused.

A hand grabbed Yael's arm and pulled her out from under the bed. She fought against him, but the grip was too hard.

'*Oi!* A little vixen!'

'Hold her tight.'

'Ach! She bit me.'

'Wait. I know her . . . '

The voice trailed off. Startled, Yael looked up. The man holding her was young, perhaps no more than twenty. His thin face was covered in mud and beneath his eyes were deep shadows. His cheeks were sunken, his chin unshaven. The other man was older. Grey hair flowed down to the collar of his coat, a military one of the style worn by the Polish army in the Great War. He had a large moustache that drooped over his mouth, giving him a hangdog expression, matched by watery blue eyes.

It was the third that had spoken. He was standing close to the door, peering at her, the rifle held loosely in his hands. He was younger even than the one holding her, his face was clean and his hair combed carefully to one side. He looked neat, despite the old and ragged clothes

'Who is she?' the older man said.

Behind them Aleksei stood in the doorway. The three partisans seemed to have forgotten him. He tried to push past the young man, but the rifle, which he was reluctant to touch, blocked his way.

'We were in the forest together for a while,' the young man said, and it was only then Yael recognised him, with a sudden leap of her heart. The young partisan paused and glanced at the older one. Yael tried to interpret the look on his face, but could not.

'With Rivka,' he said, then. 'She was with Rivka.'

The older man nodded at this. He looked hard at Yael, glancing from head to foot in a long look of appraisal. Yael felt the blood rise in her cheeks. The blush embarrassed her and she set her jaw and whipped her arm suddenly from the hand of the partisan.

'Nu,' he held the expression, so that it escaped like a long sigh. 'So you were with Rivka Plotink were you?'

Yael opened her mouth to speak, but before she got a chance, the young man spoke again.

'That's it!' he said, as if something had been troubling him and he had just thought of it. 'She is Josef's sister. You know . . . Josef . . . The one . . . '

'Josef?' Yael cried, unable to hold back. 'You know Josef? Have you seen him? Is he alive?'

The older partisan held up his hand, silencing her. He shook his head slowly, and began to turn away from her.

'Tell me please,' Yael begged, reaching out and grabbing his arm.

The partisan turned on her ferociously, so she let go and stumbled backwards, falling to the floor. Yael noticed Aleksei flinch. She worried he would launch himself at the men. Catching his eye, she shook her head. For a moment the man stood over her, his watery blue eyes glaring, but then he seemed to soften. He held out his hand and helped her to her feet.

'I'm sorry,' he said, magnanimously. 'You must understand . . . ' But he trailed off and did not tell her what it was she was to understand.

He turned to go back into the kitchen, pushing past the two younger partisans and Aleksei, who lingered in the doorway. By Aleksei's shoulder he paused and turned back. His features struggled to remain calm.

'And Rivka?' he said finally. 'You know what became of her?'

Yael met his cool eyes. She thought she saw the muscles tighten around them, barely perceptibly.

'She died,' Yael whispered. His eyes did not leave hers. She felt the full intensity of his gaze. Unexpectedly she felt a gush of sympathy for him. Of warmth.

'In the woods not far from here,' she continued, her voice little more than a whisper. 'She was sick. Some kind of fever. I woke up in the morning and she had gone.'

But he had turned away and disappeared

into the kitchen. The two younger partisans followed him. The boy paused a moment in the doorway, then stepped a pace closer to her.

'He is alive,' he whispered. 'Your brother. I haven't seen him, but I have heard of him. He commands a platoon of forest fighters.'

He was about to say more, but the older man called from outside. The young man nodded and hurried out through the kitchen. Yael sat back on the bed. Her hands were shaking. She placed them on her knees, but found they were shaking too. Her whole body juddered and suddenly she was crying. The tears flowed down her cheeks. Her nose began to run. She buried her face in her hands and wept. Josef was alive. She said the words to herself, over and over. She said them out loud, revelling in the sound of the phrase on her salty lips.

'He's alive,' she cried. Then laughed. 'He's alive.'

16

Autumn dragged. The leaves turned crisp in the dry weather. There were days when summer reasserted itself, warm bright afternoons when it seemed it would linger forever. And then, suddenly, it was November and cold, a biting edge to the wind. They woke to frosts. The brittle, sharp expiration of winter. The first dry flakes of snow that danced in the wind and settled in corners, like scraps of paper on market day.

As the weather grew worse, the visits from the small bands of partisans grew more frequent. Often it was one of the three men who had first approached them. They were polite and always asked rather than demanding, or stealing, though it would have been easy enough for them to have opened the hencoop and help themselves, or to come in with their rifles slung over their shoulders and take the bread, the hung meat, the jar of milk, the slab of butter as they wished.

To begin with Aleksei dealt with them, briskly, giving them whatever they asked for. But Yael, hungry for news of her brother and anxious about their supplies for the winter, increasingly shooed him away and bargained with the young men herself. She found she was adept at dealing with them, flirting mildly, delighting in having somebody to talk to. She would promise meat if they were able to give her the slightest bit of information about Josef. But by the end of December she had learned little more than she had from that first conversation. Josef had deserted the Red Army and was leading a platoon of partisans in the deep woods in White Russia, or Suvalki. He had developed a reputation as a commander of daring raids and his men were said to be fiercely loyal to him.

'Is it possible to get a message through to him?' Yael begged the young partisan.

The boy shrugged. Sitting at the table in an overcoat at least three times too big for him and in boots he had stolen from a dead German soldier, he looked little more than a boy, his scarlet ears sticking out. He held a steaming cup of broth in his hands and was reluctant to draw his face from the warm steam. Yael noticed the moisture condensing on his chapped lips and caked nostrils.

'There is communication,' he said finally, 'between different groups. Attempts to organise us into an army, but nobody can ever decide who is in control.' He shrugged again, as if it was all the same to him.

Yael pushed an envelope across the table. Josef's name was written neatly on the front of it. The boy looked at it nervously.

'Look-'

'Please.' Yael reached across the table and placed a hand on his sleeve. 'It's important to me.'

Seeing the boy was unconvinced, she got up and crossed to the larder.

'It's not that I don't want to help,' the boy mumbled, from inside the cup. 'It's just I don't see it getting through.'

She placed the smoked sausage in front of him. It was four inches long and two inches in diameter. Its surface crenulated and dark. She took a knife and sliced it thinly. The scent of the meat saturated the air. The boy put down the cup. Wiped at his lips carelessly as the saliva pooled in his mouth. He glanced across at Yael, who nodded.

'Have a taste,' she said.

He picked up the slice of sausage delicately between his finger and thumb and lay it on his tongue. His eyes closed and a look akin to ecstasy spread across his face. It was the kind of look on Aleksei's face, occasionally, when they made love. For a whole minute, he willed himself not to chew. Dribble spilt from between his lips. Then his jaw moved. Slowly, carefully, he crushed the sausage between his teeth, grinding the flavour from it.

'I haven't eaten meat for about six months,' he said, when he had finished. 'And that was only scraps I peeled from some bones we found discarded.'

'Take it,' she said.

He nodded his thanks, and carefully wrapped the sausage into a filthy handkerchief, putting it in an inside pocket of his coat, as if it were a holy relic entrusted to his care. He picked up the envelope too and folded it neatly and slipped it into the pocket of his shirt, not far from the sausage.

'Thank you,' Yael said.

'There's little chance . . . '

* * *

For some weeks after the young partisan left, Yael woke each morning hopeful. Often she would linger by the window, gazing out at the thickening clouds, at the slow falling snow, across the deepening drifts towards the woods. The temperature had dropped and the partisans seemed to have moved on, or dug in, because for weeks there were no more visitors to the farm.

Yael pictured her letter passing through hands, one partisan to another, travelling north, through the snow-bound woods, tucked in men's pockets as they trekked by night, until at last it would reach Josef. She imagined him waking one morning to a shout and stumbling out from the small woodcutter's cottage where his division of resistance fighters had taken shelter for the winter, to find a cold and exhausted partisan stopped by the watch. He would salute and the young man would take the envelope from his pocket, dog-eared now and pass it over to Josef.

'A letter?' Josef would mumble, rubbing the sleep from his eyes, as he always did at the breakfast table when he emerged from bed late, so caked with sleep that Yael wondered sometimes how he made it to the kitchen. And then he would see the writing. He would look up startled.

'Where did you get this?'

'It was passed on by a partisan.'

'What is it Comrade?' the watch would ask, noting the look on his face.

She could picture Josef turning the letter over, examining it like it was some miracle that had fallen into his hands.

'It's from Yael,' he would whisper. 'From my sister.'

*   *   *

Aleksei came up and stood behind her, wrapping his arms around her, and she leaned her head against his chest and together they gazed across the field and waited for the partisans who no longer came.

★   ★   ★

It was late February when Yael heard a soft scrape against the kitchen door. Aleksei had trekked into Selo, attempting to exchange some farming equipment for sugar and butter and bread. They had only a couple of chickens since the confiscation of the pigs. Yael knew he would not be back for a few days.

At first she thought it was an animal scratching around at the door, and fearing it was a wolf, she ensured it was tightly bolted. Standing close behind the door, she listened to the sounds of movement in the snow on the low step outside. Her heart lurched. She was always nervous when Aleksei was away. When she heard the soft knock, she almost cried out.

At first she tried to convince herself the animal had knocked something against the wood, but a few moments later the knock was repeated, a little stronger, a tight rhythmic beat, unmistakably human, almost domestic.

Yael stumbled back to the table and slumped on a stool, her eyes fixed upon the door, her pulse racing. Around the sides of the door, it was possible in places to see the light glinting where it did not fit tightly. Here, now, she saw the flicker of a shadow.

'Please,' a voice said in Polish. Hollow, desperate, like a whisper from beyond the grave.

Yael shrank to her knees and continued to stare at the door. She had almost convinced herself her ears had deceived her, when the unmistakable voice whispered its plea again. Getting up, she shot back the bolts and pulled open the door, her hands trembling as she hurried.

17

The figure curled in the doorway was almost unrecognisable, her hair lank and greasy, pulled severely off her face. A large coat was wrapped around her, hiding most of her face, but the sores were clearly visible.

Yael sank to her knees. Her heart thudded. She reached out a hand, but almost immediately drew it back again.

'Eva?' she whispered.

The girl in the doorway looked back at her. She was too weak to answer. Stretching out a thin hand, she attempted to grasp Yael's dress. Instinctively Yael drew back. Her mind baulked at Eva's prone body, skeletal, pale, her skin almost translucent, the veins running dark beneath the tissue-thin surface, yet she was breathing.

'I thought . . . ' Yael stammered.

The image of Eva with the others, with her parents in the forests by the pits, flashed across her mind. She gasped and felt the darkness opening up beneath her. Staggering, she put her hand out to balance herself.

An icy wind skimmed across the crust of snow and buffeted the house. Eva winced, her delicate features screwing up as though the cold was no longer bearable. In the distance a wolf howled. Yael took Eva's hands and pulled her to her feet. So icy were her fingers, Yael shivered.

Eva seemed barely able to walk. Yael led her stumbling across the kitchen and into the bedroom. She laid her on the bed and covered her with a blanket. Immediately Eva closed her eyes, sinking into the softness. Sitting beside her, Yael could feel the cold creeping through the blanket. She found another cover and laid it over the first. On top of that she laid Aleksei's coat. Eva did not stir. Her eyes remained closed. Yael might have believed she was dead, except that, plucking up the courage, she lowered herself level with Eva's face and brought herself close enough to her lips to feel the gentle stir of breath upon her cheek.

Yael got up and went to boil some water and made a thin broth from some leftover bones. Eva was sleeping so deeply, so calmly, Yael did not want to wake her. She put the cup on the floor and cleared her throat. The steam rose in the cool evening air. Yael hoped the scent of the broth would rouse her, but she didn't stir.

When Yael woke in the morning she found Eva's eyes were open, coolly regarding her.

'You're awake!' she said stupidly.

Eva did not respond. Yael sat up and reached out and touched Eva's forehead. Her temperature was still cool, but more normal than it had been the night before.

'How are you feeling?' Yael asked.

'Better,' Eva whispered.

Her voice was hoarse as though it was painful to talk. She closed her eyes briefly, then opened them again. Yael marvelled at how beautiful Eva's eyes were. Even now. They were light, hazel, flecked with gold, framed thickly with dark lashes. Despite being visibly malnourished and dirty, her face was still attractive, and her lips, though colourless, were full and moist.

Eva had sat in front of Yael in the small schoolroom. They had not been friends, though Yael would have liked that. Many afternoons she had sat gazing at Eva's long hair, enraptured with the amount of colours in it as the sun fell heavily through dusty windows. She had day-dreamed that Josef would fall in love with her and then Eva would notice her and they would be like sisters.

'You must be hungry?'

Eva nodded, her eyes widening slightly at the thought of eating. Getting up, Yael took the cup of broth she had left by the bed and poured it back into the pan that rested on the edge of the stove. She opened the cast-iron door and rekindled the fire, pushing fresh log chips into it. When it was hot enough, she latched the door and moved the pan across to the ring, from which she removed the metal covering, so the flames licked the bottom of the thick black pot. While it was heating up, she took a couple of buckets and collected snow to melt for water, and pulled the tin tub out into the middle of the kitchen.

Eva was sitting up in bed when Yael came in with the steaming cup and a crust of bread. She took the broth and drank it greedily, wincing at its heat.

'Eat slowly,' Yael counselled her, quietly. 'It will make you sick if you haven't eaten for a while.'

Eva flashed her a look that quietened her. She laughed a low, guttural, ironic chuckle. The heat of the broth had flushed her cheeks, and she looked immediately stronger, invigorated.

'Don't you worry about me,' Eva said. 'I've managed.'

'You look thin.'

'I'm not the fat one,' Eva said, eyeing her. 'Never have been! *Got-tse-dánken!*' She reached out and placed the tips of her fingers on Yael's sleeve, removing them almost instantly.

Yael looked down at the floor. In the time she had spent in Aleksei's house, she had grown. She had put on some weight, despite, or perhaps because of the limited diet she and Aleksei lived on. The weight had not gone exactly where she would have preferred, so that her breasts remained quite small, whilst her hips and thighs were thicker. Looking in the mirror, she had been pleased to see that her body was becoming womanly, but now she felt suddenly self-conscious under Eva's gaze.

She stood up and straightened her clothes. She was wearing a collarless shirt and a pair of Aleksei's trousers, which she held up with an old pair of his braces, and a belt, in which she had had to punch new holes. She took the cup from Eva.

'Is there more?' Eva asked.

'Of course,' Yael whispered.

In the kitchen she regarded herself in the sliver of mirror. Her face was plain besides Eva's, her eyes dully dark, lips less full. Despite Eva's emaciated state, the dirt under her broken fingernails, her greasy, matted hair, she still bore about her an air of glamour.

'I'm heating up some water,' Yael said,

when she took through the cup of broth. 'You can have a wash.'

Eva nodded. She took the cup and sipped the broth more slowly, savouring it, dipping the crust of bread and allowing it to dissolve on her tongue. For some time they sat in silence. Eva examined Yael frankly, taking in the clothes, the changes in her body, her hair, which was clean and tied back loosely with a scarf.

'I didn't expect to find you here,' she said finally.

'I thought you were dead,' Yael blurted.

Eva simply shook her head. Her eyes did not leave Yael's. She did not seem to want to talk about what had happened. Yael did not either; the very thought of what had happened in the woods filled her with horror. Nevertheless, she felt an uncontrollable urge to know. Just to know.

'This house,' Eva said, interrupting Yael's thoughts, 'I was lost, but when I came out on the road up there and looked down at the house, I thought I recognised it.'

'We're not far from Selo,' Yael agreed. 'It's about ten kilometres away.'

'This house though,' Eva continued, 'Isn't it the crazy guy's?'

'Yes . . . no . . . I mean he's not mad, he's not crazy, really . . . He just can't speak.'

'Where is he?'

'He's gone to Selo to buy some goods.'

'He's sheltering you?'

'Yes.'

Eva thought about this. Yael could almost see the thought process moving across her face.

'For how long?'

'I've been here about a year now.'

'You've been here a year and nobody has given you in?'

'Nobody comes here, Aleksei doesn't communicate much with the world.'

Eva nodded. She drained the broth and handed Yael the empty cup. Sitting up, she swung her feet down to the floor. Her stockings were threadbare, her toes poked through holes in the tattered cloth, black with dirt and stained from the shoes she had been wearing.

'I need to wash!' she said emphatically.

* * *

While Yael heated up the water, Eva undressed carefully. She showed no embarrassment in front of Yael. Glancing up, Yael found her stood naked beside her. Her ribs showed clearly, her skin was dark with dirt, marked by the track of lice and in places sores marked her skin angrily. Still she was beautiful. She gasped when she stepped in the water.

'Oh!' she said. And then again, 'Oh, you cannot know, you cannot begin to know how that feels.'

Yael smiled, pleased, and yet still she felt a sharp, little twinge of irritation that Eva seemed adamant she could not know how good the water felt. She recalled almost a year ago how she had felt stepping for the first time into the bathtub. Something that even now, a year later, she could not take for granted.

Taking a jug from the kitchen shelf, Yael poured warm water down over Eva's long dark hair. She scrubbed her head hard with soap, rinsed it with hot water, then combed it through with a fine-toothed comb Aleksei had bought for her on a previous trip into Selo. The water in the tub was soon black, and Yael urged Eva out. She wrapped her in towels, heated more water and poured a new bath.

For three hours Yael bathed her, combing through her hair again and again, pulling out lice by the handful, cutting back her ragged nails and cleaning the dirt from beneath them, tending to the bruises and cuts and sores on her flesh. By lunchtime Eva's flesh shone pink from where it had been scrubbed.

Her hair glistened in the light from the window. She smelled of soap. Yael combed her hair into one thick plait that hung down her neck, showing off the elegant narrow curve of her throat and her defined, small shoulders. She dabbed perfume on her skin.

'Yael, you will never know how good it is possible to feel!' Eva declared with a grin.

Yael smiled, glad to see Eva so happy. She was radiantly beautiful. She pushed the naked girl through into the bedroom, and indicated the wardrobe.

'Find yourself some clean clothes to wear,' she said. 'I'll try to wash some of your clothes and see if they are salvageable.'

Piling Eva's old clothes on the table, she threw away the underwear and stockings which were beyond repair. She examined the dress, but that was so infested with lice that in places it seemed as if the material had been stitched together from living things. Disgusted, she took the clothes and fed them all into the fire of the stove. She began to prepare some food when Eva stepped back into the room.

Yael started. Eva was dressed in the flowered silk blouse and trim black skirt Aleksei had kept wrapped in brown packaging. The clothes fitted her well. With her hair pulled back from her face, her skin pink from

117

the hot bath, she looked elegant. As if she had just stepped off a Parisian street.

'Eva . . . ' Yael stuttered.

A sound at the door caused both girls to turn at once. The door opened and silhouetted against the bright snow, Aleksei stood, a box cradled in his hands.

18

Aleksei stopped in the doorway. Yael saw the look of fright slither across his face. He took in the clothes and glanced at Yael, a quick, flashing glance that spoke of incomprehension and betrayal.

'Aleksei . . . ' Yael dropped the wooden spoon with which she had been stirring a thick soup. It landed with a clatter on the wooden floorboards.

Eva stepped forward to meet Aleksei on the threshold. Yael was startled at her easy confidence.

'Hello,' she said, with a smile, in slow, well-enunciated Polish, such as one might use to a child.

Aleksei stepped back a pace, but Eva had already taken the box from his arms, and lifted it easily onto the kitchen table. She turned her back on Aleksei, as if he were of no further interest, as if there could be nothing odd in her sudden appearance in his house.

'Look Yael,' she said, delighted, 'just look what he has brought, your crazy goy.' She addressed Yael in Yiddish.

Yael hurried to Aleksei and pulled him in, closing the door. She could feel him shaking.

'Her name is Eva,' Yael said softly, guiding him across to the chair and sitting him down, peeling the cold overcoat off him. 'We were at school together. I found her on the doorstep last night. She was freezing. She would have died if I had left her out there. I'm sorry about the clothes, I didn't know.' She found she was gabbling and this was upsetting him more.

Eva looked up. 'I'm sorry,' she said smiling, 'I didn't introduce myself . . . it was just the sight of this food! You don't know what the sight of sausage means to a young girl these days!' she joked. She held out her thin, clean, elegant hand. Instinctively, almost like a child, Aleksei held out his. He glanced up nervously, as Eva held onto it for a moment. She appraised him coolly, openly, an eyebrow rising ironically. Yael wondered that she could have remained so vivacious.

An old familiar feeling shuddered through Yael, and at once she felt as though she was back at school. She felt with painful clarity her girlish idolisation of Eva, her envy of the older girl's beauty, her desire for acknowledgement, the bruising knowledge of her insignificance in her presence.

She turned to Eva now, gathering herself.

'Those clothes, Eva, I didn't mean them. They are special. They . . . '

Aleksei waved his hand, stopping her. Yael felt her heart shift a little. Aleksei stood up. He paused a moment, glancing at both girls, then turned away from the table and went through to the bedroom, where he kicked off his boots and lay on the bed, his back turned to the kitchen door.

'Is he all right?' Eva mouthed. 'He looked a bit put out.'

'He's not used to company,' Yael whispered.

* * *

She boiled some water and made some sweet tea and took it through to Aleksei, but he did not turn to her when she settled down on the edge of the bed. When she laid a hand on his shoulder, he shrugged her off. His eyes were closed firmly and he would not open them. For some time Yael sat beside him, stroking his arm softly. From the kitchen she could hear sounds of Eva bustling around, stirring the soup and then brushing the floor.

'You shouldn't,' Yael said, coming through into the kitchen. 'You need to rest, to get your strength back.'

'I feel fine,' Eva grinned.

Later that evening Yael made up a bed on the floor in the kitchen and she and Eva settled down there. Glancing through the doorway into the bedroom, she longed to be by Aleksei's side, to feel him by her, to wrap her arms around his body and fall asleep against him, but she felt she could not do this in front of Eva. Eva's presence had unsettled everything and she could not help but feel a sharp sense of resentment.

'It was all so sudden,' Eva murmured in the darkness as they lay side by side on the kitchen floor. 'We were all convinced we were going to Plotsk, that the Germans were simply removing us from the battlefront. There was some talk of ghettos, that we were being taken to work camps, like those in Germany. Some of the men had spoken of making a break for it, of trying to overpower the guards, but then other's argued it would be dangerous. Far better to wait until we were in Plotsk, and then see what the situation was. Think of the older ones, somebody said, they won't be able to escape into the forests. And the little ones, somebody else said.

'When we were a few kilometres outside Selo they stopped the column. Even then there was no hint of what was to come. We were directed off the road. Some of the men began to get restless. Michael Leizer and some others started shouting. One boy, one of the Lieberwitzes I think, made a break for the forest. They shot him. That was when we began to get scared.

'I held my mother's hand. She kept whispering, 'Don't worry, it's all right, there's nothing to worry about.' She couldn't stop. Even when we were down in the bottom of that god-awful pit and they were digging the holes, throwing the spades at us, she kept on and on.

'I can't even remember what I was thinking. We're going to die, I think. Just that, over and over again, we're going to die, while my mother kept saying, 'It's going to be all right, don't worry.' Even when they started shooting. Even after the shooting had started and people were falling down all around us, she stood there, her hand crushing mine, whispering, 'It's going to be fine, don't worry, my love, it's going to be all right.'

'Then I was down on the floor. There were bodies on top of me. I didn't know if I had been shot. I lay there as the bodies crushed me. I was soaking wet and I didn't realise it was blood — that I was soaked from head to toe in blood. I lay there with my eyes squeezed tight.

'Then the shooting stopped. For some time it was quiet. Totally silent. And then the breeze picked up in the tops of the trees and I heard the sound of birds again and some men muttering. I didn't move. Not a muscle. I lay there, trying not to breathe. The men were poking around and then I heard a gun shot. Isolated shots. Like they were picking off the last of the dying.

'Later they started to throw earth over the bodies. It got dark. For hours they worked and then I started panicking that I was going to be buried alive and I didn't know what to do, to start trying to get out or to stay there. The weight on top of me was crushing. It was hard to breathe. The blood had started to dry and it was sticky and my skin itched. I twitched my fingers and found that they were still clasped in Mama's. I moved them, trying to pass a message to her, trying to see if she was still alive too, but there was nothing. Her hands were cold, but so were mine, and my nerves were crushed and I had pins and needles, so it was hard to tell much.

'It was late, very late, when I started to move. They had stopped shovelling. I hadn't heard their shouts for quite a while. I lost track of time. The sky was dark though. I inched myself up, struggling to move without making a sound. It seemed like an hour or two before I managed to move more than a foot. The layer of soil was thin over the top of the bodies. As far as I could tell there was nobody around, but I couldn't be sure the Germans hadn't left some guards. I slid across the bodies into the undergrowth. There were others there. The forest floor seemed to be alive with Jews slithering along on their bellies like snakes.'

She stopped. Yael glanced at her face. It was expressionless. Eva gazed up at the ceiling, her hands folded across her breasts. She looked calm and collected, but under the sheet Yael could feel her body shaking, a tight, rapid vibration. Yael moved closer and stroked her forehead, smoothing her hair away from her face. Eva turned and smiled at her softly.

'My parents?' Yael whispered. 'Did you see anything of them?'

'No, Yael,' Eva whispered. 'I'm sorry, I didn't.'

★   ★   ★

On that day Yael had arranged to hike with a group of friends to a lake and when they backed out she decided to go on her own. It had been a willful action, but the weather had been fine and bright and she had enjoyed the time alone. It was late afternoon, as she was returning, when she bumped into a farmer the family knew. He had looked at her as though she was a ghost. He took her arm and pulled her to the side of the track and she had been scared.

'Go!' he had whispered hoarsely at her. 'They are taking everybody.'

It had meant nothing to her. She had shrugged him off, pulling her arm away. She hurried back along the path through the trees, towards the town.

When she joined the main road it was quiet. The sun was beginning to fall. By the side of the road was a suitcase. It had been dropped and the clasps had come undone and the clothes spilled out on the verge; a cream blouse, women's underwear. A darkness stirred inside her. Further down there was another bundle. A dog was nosing at it and each time it moved a dark cloud would rise into the air above.

She recognised the woman. It was Abigail, the baker's wife. She had a large hole where one of her eyes had been. Flies buzzed. Her whole face was crawling. Yael bent over and retched. The sound of an engine startled her. Turning around she saw an army truck driving out from the woods and down the road in her direction. Instinctively she ducked into the darkness of the trees and watched as it passed. In the back the men were drinking; their faces were hard and dark and their eyes stared blankly. One of the men cracked a joke and the others laughed mirthlessly.

It was the next day that she had run into Rivka in the forest.

After that, everything had changed.

19

Eva took extraordinary care over her appearance, Yael thought. She watched as the elder girl conducted her ablutions the next morning. Yael had slept badly on the thin covers on the kitchen floor and woke with a headache and a sore throat. Eva, however, declared she had not slept so well in months. Yael brewed some tea, a cup of which she carried through to Aleksei. He nodded his thanks to her and for this she was grateful and rested her forehead against his briefly.

Before dressing, Eva washed carefully. If she was aware of Aleksei's presence she showed no signs of being bothered by him.

'In the forest, there was little room for modesty,' she explained.

Yael sat at the table. Eva pulled up the hem of the shirt she had slept in and bathed her shapely thighs, as she threw back her head so her dark hair cascaded down her back, and wiped her long throat with the damp cloth. Aleksei glanced up, then looked away startled and embarrassed. But Yael noticed his eyes flick back occasionally, as if caught on strings and yanked, without his willing it, in Eva's direction.

'Eva,' Yael whispered, and nodded in Aleksei's direction.

'Oh I'm sure he's seen worse!' Eva laughed.

She dressed carefully in the clothes from the brown paper package; the silk blouse that fitted her neatly, accentuating her breasts, the skirt which displayed her small waist.

'Yael, sweety!' she said. 'Help me with my hair.'

★   ★   ★

Over the next few days, despite her reluctance, Yael enjoyed having a girl's company. Eva was happy to talk, and as they worked together, cleaning the house, they shared memories of Selo, of school and the friends they had. Eva told her about life in the woods; of how there were whole families surviving in the wild, three generations of a family, living in a narrow dugout, like frightened rabbits. She talked of the partisans she had come across.

But as the days passed Yael felt the house shrink. Life was circumscribed by Eva's presence. Aleksei was agitated. Often he would storm out of the farmhouse and she would worry that he would disappear, but he would come back an hour or so later and linger in the doorway, watching them.

Yael longed for the silence of her life with Aleksei. The quiet hours when they would look out across the snow-bound fields, listening to the sound of one another breathing. When the feel of his hand, not more than an inch or two from hers, would make her shiver. She longed for the books, the hours spent reading, his quiet concentration, the soft, sibilant sound of her tongue on the smooth verses.

And Eva would take little care. She would wander down to the well in the daytime and linger there, staring out into the woods. Aleksei would stand by the window, clearing his throat, scratching at the skin on his arms. He seemed to fear confronting her, and did not go out to remonstrate silently with her, as he had with Yael. It was Yael who scuttled out, nervous, glancing up towards the road, to see that nobody passing by would see them.

'Eva come in,' Yael begged, in a low voice, tugging at the sleeve of the coat she wore.

'Leave me.'

'It's not safe, Eva.'

'Don't order me around,' Eva turned on her viciously. Her eyes were alive and fierce. Yael was stung by the sharpness of her tongue.

That evening Eva pulled out the tin bath and heated up some water. Yael was out in the woods gathering firewood, to supplement the logs Aleksei had cut in the summer. The quietness of the woods soothed her. Aleksei worked by her side silently. Occasionally their bodies would draw close to each other, graze as they picked up the sticks, and Yael would feel a fizz of delight sparkle across her skin. In a little clearing, they stopped in the shadow of the trees and stood gazing out at the brilliant whiteness of the moonlight on the snow. Their breath hung in frosty clouds. A fox darted across the clearing, not noticing them.

When they returned, Eva was sitting naked in the tub. Aleksei stumbled in the door and would have turned and left, but Yael coming up so close behind him not understanding why he faltered, and keen to be out of the freezing night, pushed him forward. It was not until the door was closed behind her, that she glimpsed Eva's ripe flesh and her smile like a split peach.

'Eva!'

'I didn't expect you so quickly.' Eva laughed and stepped from the tub reluctantly, reaching up to take a towel from a hook on the wall, so that her full, lovely body was on show.

Aleksei hurried through to the bedroom

and pulled closed the curtain. 'Eva, how could you?' Yael said sharply.

'What?' Eva wrapped the towel around her. 'How was I to know you would walk in? Besides,' she added tartly, 'you think he hasn't seen a woman before?'

Yael turned from her angrily.

★ ★ ★

Later, Yael heard him fumbling about. Occasionally his bed would creak as he sat on it, but he seemed unable to rest and late into the night Yael heard him pacing the small room, as Eva slept quietly beside her.

★ ★ ★

'What are your plans?' Yael asked the next morning. She attempted to keep her voice light, but the anger from the previous evening had not dissipated.

'Plans?'

They were sitting at the kitchen table, Yael stitching some old trousers of Aleksei's that had split, while Eva stared absently out through the window at the heavy layer of cloud that shrouded the sky, promising more snow. It would soon be March.

'I mean,' said Yael, searching for words,

reaching for some language that would express the confused emotions that whirled around her mind. 'I mean, how long are you thinking of staying here?'

Eva glanced sharply at Yael. Her lips tightened and Yael noticed the narrowing of her eyes.

'What do you mean by that?'

'You were talking of the partisans ... I thought ... '

Eva stood up and walked slowly around the table, stopping by the window, her back to Yael.

'I see,' she said, choosing Yiddish.

Often when they spoke, they used Polish. Yael did not like talking in front of Aleksei in a language he did not understand. Eva seemed oblivious to this courtesy and would often slip back into the colloquial language of their childhood.

'What do you mean, 'you see'?' said Yael.

Eva turned from the window.

'It's fine,' Eva said, her voice laced with contempt. 'As soon as the weather improves, I will be out of your hair. I'm not going to spend my time cooped up in this hovel. I'm going to join a partisan group and fight.'

'It's not that I don't want you here,' Yael whispered, shamed.

Eva laughed unkindly. 'I don't care! You

think I'm a threat to your little *home?*'

She pronounced the word with such contempt that Yael felt a rush of embarrassment. She stood up and faced the older girl. Eva cocked back her head and looked down her nose at Yael.

'Why are you so cruel?' Yael whispered. She had wanted to confront Eva, but the voice that emerged was timid.

'Me? I am the cruel one?'

'Why do you behave like this?'

'You are a disgrace!' Eva sneered. She stormed across the room and grabbed a coat. 'I'm going. You happy? That's what you wanted, no? *Nu, va!* There you go — I'd be better off with that family in their hole in the ground, at least there I would have some self-respect.'

'Eva.'

Eva took off her skirt and grabbed the mended trousers from the table. She pulled these on and slipped her feet into boots.

'Don't be silly, Eva.'

Grabbing a scarf and a hat, which she pushed forcibly down over her hair, Eva just grunted. She pulled open the door.

'Eva, come back!'

Eva threw a crude comment over her shoulder as she stomped away from the house.

Yael felt a sudden rush of fury at the young woman. She picked up a small log and threw it out after her. Eva turned and the wood hit her on the forehead. She yelped in pain. A thin trickle of blood ran down her face. Wildly, they stared at each other, their breath curdling in the frosty air. Yael was shocked at her own temper. The ferocity with which she felt when protecting Aleksei and the life they had together. Eva turned and slowly walked away in the direction of the edge of the forest.

'Eva!'

'May you rot in hell!'

Her voice drifted back across the snow. Yael fell to her knees on the doorstep, a sob rising in her chest. She watched until the figure disappeared between the trees.

'Eva,' she cried. Her voice echoed back from the forest wall, bringing Aleksei running from the front field where he had been mending a fence.

'She's gone,' Yael wailed, as he stooped down and grabbed her. 'Go after her, Aleksei, go fetch her back.'

But Aleksei lifted her from the doorstep and carried her inside. She pushed against him, struggling to be free of his arms, but he held tight to her. He carried her through to the bedroom and laid her gently on the bed. When she struggled to get up, crying, the tears choking back her words, he shook his head and held his fingers against her lips.

'We can't just let her go,' Yael cried.

But Aleksei held her there, until finally her sobbing had stopped and her body had ceased to shake. She lay quietly as he sat beside her and stroked her hair. They did not move for the whole afternoon and soon the sun had set. Aleksei brought her bread cut thick and clumsily, and a sliver of cheese. She ate it hungrily. He lay beside her then and took her in his arms and she buried her face in his chest.

'I am evil,' Yael whispered in the darkness.

But Aleksei had no words for her.

20

The stork brings spring upon its tail, the saying goes — *Bocian na ogonie jaskółkę przynosi*. It was mid-March when one landed in the field, and stood there almost motionless as Yael gazed through the window. She recalled her father telling her that when the storks flew down to Africa for the winter, they took the longer route down across Palestine, rather than crossing the Mediterranean. The journey was longer, but it was easier for the stork because of the way it flew. Its large wings were clumsy and heavy to flap, which made crossing the sea, with its turbulent wind currents, difficult, whereas flying down across the land, the bird barely had to move, riding the warm air.

She imagined this bird now having wintered in Jaffa, in the marshy plains of Palestine, along the reed beds of the Nile. An exotic, far-off world, beyond belief on this little farm, penned in by winter and war.

The bird was tall, a metre high with long, thin legs, a white head, neck and body and black wing feathers. Around each eye was a small patch of dark skin. Suddenly, as Yael watched, its neck twitched and then jabbed forward towards the earth, rising a moment or two later, with a small rodent trembling in its beak.

As Aleksei made his way outside, he paused by her side for a moment to see what she was looking at. Seeing the stork, he smiled and wrapped his arm around her. Bending slightly, he pointed up to the top of a wooden pole before the house. On the top of it were the crumbling remains of a nest.

'Do you think they will nest there this year?' Yael asked.

Aleksei smiled.

* * *

Since Eva had gone, Yael had slept badly. Each night she was troubled by dreams of the young woman lost in dark forests, ensnared by German soldiers. She dreamt of the pit in the woods, of creeping between dead bodies, of movement stiffened by the congealed blood that coated her. Often she would wake with a cry and Aleksei would sit up to find her wide-eyed, hair lank with sweat, trembling.

The stork began work repairing the nest at the top of the large pole by the house, bringing twigs and small branches from the forest. Later he brought moss and grass and even old newspaper found blowing around outside the house to line the nest. The nest was an old one, and it had grown over the years to almost two metres in diameter. Several other storks had taken up residence in the close vicinity and Yael fondly watched them establishing their homes with such care. It cheered her to think it was only humans that were fighting this war, that the birds and the wild animals could continue to exist as they always had. Life continued to go on.

'Oh that I really was vermin,' she said to Aleksei one evening as they sat in darkness by the stove, watching the flames of the furnace glittering through the slightly opened door. 'I wish I was a rat, scuttling about in the forest, free to live as I wished.'

By the end of March the stork was established on its nest. From the direction of the road another stork swooped slowly down out of the sky. The bright morning sunlight caught its white underbelly, the wide span of its black wings, illuminated its startling red beak. The male in the nest crouched down and began shaking its head, spreading out its six-foot wingspan. The newly arrived settled down on the edge of the nest, its wings still spread wide, imitating its nodding — first from side to side, then perceptibly up and down. Their beaks clattered loudly.

Yael, watching, felt a wave of joy sparkle down her spine. She shivered. The stork cannot sing, her father had told her once, in fact they are more or less mute.

'What do you mean?'

'You listen to them, they can't sing. All they can manage upon occasion is a hiss.'

'Why is that?' Yael had asked.

But her father was only able to shake his head. 'I'm not a scientist,' he grumbled pleasantly, ruffling her hair, 'that's how God made them, even the females!' He laughed. 'It was a blessing,' he added.

'My little stork,' he called her. 'My quiet one.'

Yael imagined being a stork. Imagined opening wide her wings and dropping down off that large nest, allowing the wind to gather beneath her wings, sailing up over the trees, over the top of the forest, following rivers, down across the continent, stopping briefly in the Ukraine and feasting on its rich harvest, over the cupolas and spires of Sofia, settling among the minarets of Istanbul. Poking around in the foothills of Hermon, wading in the shallows of Galilee.

Then I lifted up mine eyes, and looked, and, behold, there came out two women, and the wind was in their wings; for they had wings like the wings of a stork.

She dreamt that night she found Eva in the depths of the forest, with wings like a stork. She sailed through the morning air and settled on the edge of a nest, where another was waiting for her, bobbing its head, up and down, clacking its beak. It was Josef, she realised later, this stork in the nest. Yael called out from the grass below them, but they sailed off across the forest, leaving her there, alone.

* * *

As May passed into June and the weather grew hotter, Yael began to worry less about Eva. As long as the good weather held, she would be able to survive in the woods, Yael considered. She was probably better off, safer perhaps in the woods than in the farmhouse. She slept better, and once more felt the quiet comfort of the familiar rituals, the closely circumscribed life. She began reading to Aleksei in the evening again, settling on Pushkin.

'It's like my past is unravelling before me,' Yael said to Aleksei, laying aside the book one evening.

Aleksei looked up from the fire, his eyes questioning.

'I have nothing to do here and cannot imagine what might come. It's like the future and present have been taken from me, and I'm left only with memories. Sometimes I can picture them, as clear and tangible as if they were here — or rather, I was there. I feel I could reach out and touch them.

'Some mornings I wake, and before I open my eyes, I imagine I am back in my bed at home and Josef is close by and I can hear my father walking around and mother is cooking some porridge for breakfast. I can smell it. Occasionally I close my eyes and picture Josef and can hear his voice exactly. Exactly. Is it possible that it's gone?'

Aleksei held out his hand to her.

'But is it possible that it could be taken away so quickly? That a whole world could be erased like a mistake in a school book, and that nobody will protest? Is it possible to do that?'

Aleksei bowed his head.

'But what will they do?' Yael continued. 'The barber was Jewish, the factory owner. Zalman Lunski who owned the only truck to take the farmer's produce to Plotsk. How will they do anything with no Jews?'

Aleksei got up and poured water into the blackened kettle that he placed onto the stove. It sizzled as the flames licked the moisture along the bottom. Yael watched his quiet movements, studied the broad slope of his back, the muscles in his arms, the dark long hair that fell down across his cheeks.

'Why don't you talk?' she said. 'What happened, Aleksei, that stopped you from speaking?'

He paused, hand above the kettle as though about to remove it, though it was a long way from boiling. He half turned, but then stopped. His fingers tightened and then relaxed. He reached up and tucked the hair back off his face and walked across the kitchen to fetch two cups; new ones he had brought back from Selo on his last visit. They were made from fine china, with a flowered pattern in pink and green worming its way around the rim. Like the ones the Leizer family had.

*   *   *

The female stork on the nest had laid her eggs and the two birds made regular trips out across the fields to find food. From the window Yael watched them, marvelling at the care shown by the large birds for their clattering young.

'That was how they gained their name in Hebrew,' her father had told her. 'Chasidah.

From *chesed*. It means kindness.'

★ ★ ★

'Nothing bad will happen to us now,' Yael whispered to Aleksei in the darkness one night. 'You know the saying? Lightening does not strike the nest of a stork. *Gdzie bocian na gnieździe, tam piorun nie uderzy.* They will keep us safe, our family of storks.'

★ ★ ★

The next day the Germans came.

21

Aleksei woke first. A thin grey light seeped through the curtains. A dog barked, but that was not what woke him. He shook Yael, who mumbled and turned over. Pushing her again, he took her shoulder and shook her fiercely.

'What is it?' she murmured, drawing herself up from a deep well of sleep. Aleksei indicated for her to listen. 'It's only a dog,' she said after a moment and collapsed back onto the old mattress, rolling in close against his side where it was warmer.

Aleksei swung his legs over the side of the bed and ran a hand through his hair. An engine was running somewhere, up on the road at the top of the path. Yael groaned and reached out a hand to restrain him.

'It's too early.'

The bang on the door startled them both. Yael sat up sharply, her eyes widening, suddenly awake. Half standing, Aleksei seemed unsure which way to turn. At that moment, behind them, there was a sharp tap on the glass of the window. A small, soft shriek escaped Yael's lips. She dropped back onto the mattress pulling the sheet across her.

Aleksei bent down and grabbed her arm. He pulled her up and out of the bed. Pushing aside the clothes in the wardrobe, he inched open the false partition and roughly pushed Yael through. The darkness enfolded her. She stood bolt upright, her heart pounding and her body shaking so much she feared the whole wardrobe would start rattling.

'Hey!' a voice called from the doorway.

Yael heard Aleksei's feet slap across the floorboards, the struggled noises he made when afraid, attempts at speech. Boots clumped across the kitchen and into the bedroom. Their voices were so close, Yael felt she was stood among them. She heard the creak of the bed and someone's voice, squeezed, as they bent double, checking beneath it. The door of the wardrobe clicked open and she heard the sound of heavy breathing, the swish of clothes on hangers, fingernails scratching against the thin plywood. A stream of light split the darkness of her compartment, falling upon her hand. Yael trembled, felt her skin dampen with a cold sweat. Her head spun dizzily. The fingers scraped against her compartment and she heard a muttering not more than a foot away.

'*Nix!*'

'Nothing at all?'

'Just old clothes.'

'And these books?'

'His books?'

'They're all in Russian.'

There was a moment's silence. Yael's breathing came in shallow gulps. She closed her eyes, but nervously they sprang open again, fixed upon the dark wood no more than a few inches before her eyes. She tried to shift her feet but could not without making a noise. When she had been pressed into the space, she had not had time to arrange herself in a comfortable position and already she was finding it difficult to stand. Her legs had started to ache.

'You are a Bolshevik? A communist?' It was barked in German first, then, hesitantly in Polish with a strong accent. 'Communist?'

She heard his muttering, the guttural gurgles, the coughs and throat clearing. Heard his feet shifting.

'Well?'

'Answer the Commander!'

A hollow stamp vibrated the floorboards. The German soldiers laughed. Through the half-inch narrow gap Yael caught a glimpse of him stood in the middle of the room. His long night shirt flapped open, revealing his broad chest, his arm raised in a Nazi salute. His dark hair was wild about his head, thrown back, his eyes staring, bright with fear. In a tight semi-circle the soldiers stood around him, submachine guns slung on leather straps across their shoulders, pointed at his waist.

★ ★ ★

The soldiers settled themselves down in the kitchen. From her hiding place Yael heard the sounds of the engines of their lorries as they drove down the field, the shouted commands, the sound of feet crunching around the house. A small squad of Einsatzkommandos set up camp on the farm. A number of tents were erected on the back field. Later in the morning Yael heard the sound of a pig squealing manically, a blood-curdling sound. At midday the breeze blew in the scent of wood smoke through the house, and a little later pork frying. Aleksei ducked in and out of the house, carrying drinks, doing odd jobs, busying himself. Occasionally when he felt himself unobserved he crept into the bedroom and stood by the wardrobe. His silent desperation permeated the air.

In the narrow space Yael shifted her weight from one foot to the other. She attempted to squat down, but the compartment was not wide enough and her hips caught against the sides. She leant one way and then the other

148

but after an hour or two she felt her legs could stand it no longer. Sharp pains shot up from her calf muscles. Her thighs ached. Panic overtook her and she found she could not breathe. As wide as she opened her mouth she did not seem able to get air into her lungs. Perspiration soaked her clothes. Her body seemed to whirl in the air. Her head fell forward and cracked against the wood. She wanted to cry. She wanted to scream.

Aleksei squeezed a glass through the back of the wardrobe, easing open the partition a couple of inches. Yael drank the water quickly, but soon after found her bladder was full. For an hour she nursed it, the increasing pain forcing out any other feeling. Finally unable to hold it any longer, she allowed her muscles to relax a little, felt the warm trickle down her leg, soaking her nightdress, pooling under her feet. She cried then. Silently. Painfully. Cried from the very depth of her being.

★ ★ ★

Darkness began to fall. By then numbness had overtaken Yael. She did not cry. Nor did she particularly think. She shifted her weight from one leg to the other, counted occasionally. She tried to rouse herself at one point, to collect her thoughts, but after a few moments she gave up and allowed the blankness to envelop her once more. She went through periods when she thought she could stand the pain and the tiredness no longer, when she felt she must surely faint, but she didn't and then the point would pass, her mind would drift and time would continue.

'They can kill me,' she thought at one point. 'I'm too tired for this.' But the moment she thought it, she was disgusted with herself. Anger seeped into her bloodstream. Her muscles tautened and her nerves quivered at the thought of those who had died and she was strengthened and knew she would not let them catch her. That she at least would survive.

It was pitch black and she had dozed off when Aleksei eased open the wardrobe door and gently tapped his fingernails against the wood. Yael's eyes flickered open and she felt a tremor pass across her nerves.

'Aleksei?' she whispered, but he hushed her.

Carefully he prised open the partition. A weak light illuminated the room against which he was silhouetted. The air was cool upon her face. Yael fell forward and Aleksei caught her. Gently he lifted her out of the gap, took her in his arms and carried her across to the bed where he laid her tenderly. The relief was enormous. Her body sank into the softness of the mattress. Aleksei stroked her hair, anxiety twisting the shadows on his face. He pulled her softly, but insistently, pointing towards the door.

'Let me lay still,' she whispered, desperately. 'I can't move.'

Aleksei shook his head.

'Please,' she begged softly.

Aleksei's muscles were tight with fear. He looked wretched, Yael thought. She glanced towards the door to the kitchen, across which the curtain had been drawn.

'Are they through there?' she whispered, nodding towards the doorway.

Aleksei shook his head again, but eased her up into a sitting position. He indicated towards the window and stood and unlatched it. A cool breeze wafted through. Faintly Yael could hear the sound of talking, low voices, muttering somewhere in the darkness. Aleksei pulled her up to the window. He pointed out towards the black shadows of the forest. Wearily Yael nodded. She felt so tired she felt she would vomit if she moved again, if she had to stand once more.

Aleksei opened the window wider and leaned out. Confident no one was there, he quickly ducked back inside the room and lifted Yael up. She swung her legs over the sill and stopped a moment. Aleksei stood before her. She leant down and kissed him, then slipped down onto the ground, flattening herself against the grass.

22

The ground was dew-damp and quickly soaked through Yael's clothes. From the front of the house, she heard a commotion — a shout and the sound of angry voices. She shuffled forward, worming her way through the grass. Footsteps stopped her a moment and she saw a figure run past her in the darkness. When the soldier had gone, she moved on, as fast as she could. Her hand scraped against a stone sending a jolt of pain up her arm, but she did not pause.

When she was closer to the line of trees, and sheltered by the thick darkness, she got to her hands and knees and scuttled to the shelter of the forest. Turning, then, she looked back down the field. A fire burned brightly at the back of the house, close to the well, and its dancing light illuminated Aleksei stood against the wall, his hands folded on his head, surrounded by shouting soldiers. One moved forward and hit him hard and he staggered back and fell against the bricks. Another raised his rifle and seemed about to fire. A scream caught in Yael's throat. She stopped it with her hands, clamping them tight across her lips, sealing in the sound, so her breath rushed out through her nostrils.

Aleksei stood up slowly. The soldier lowered his gun. He shouted at Aleksei, but the moment of crisis seemed to have passed. Before he went back inside the farmhouse, Aleksei hung around by the German tents. He accepted a cigarette and wandered out into the darkness, staring into the shadows. Yael tried to wave to him, but he was looking in the wrong direction and she feared revealing herself. He turned finally, and threw the cigarette in the fire. Still he paused before entering the door. He turned one final time and Yael saw the pained expression on his face.

When he had gone, she withdrew a little into the woods, crawling into a thicket, and there, with her arms wrapped tight around herself, she slept. Sleep came surprisingly easily and was deep and seemingly dreamless. When she awoke the first stain of light was seeping across the sky. It was cold. Yael shivered, her teeth chattering, her muscles trembling uncontrollably. She looked around, unnerved by the unfamiliar, and yet all too familiar surroundings. How she wished she could crawl into the crook of Aleksei's arm, curl up tight in the warmth.

She longed to be back there at the house

with him, even in the wardrobe, stuck in the few inches of space, unable to move. Just to be back within those familiar confines, to be near Aleksei, to know he was there for her.

She crawled out from between the thickets and glanced around. A thin mist hung close to the ground, between the trunks of the trees. No breath of air stirred. The morning was preternaturally quiet. From the distance then she heard the sound of a motor cough. Her heart leapt. They're moving, was her first thought. They're going.

She scuttled through the undergrowth, crawling as she neared the edge of the forest, pausing on the lip of the hill to gaze down into the clearing where the farm stood. The milky fog was thicker in the hollow. At first only the roof of the house was visible, and the chimney, a thin plume of smoke rising from it. The engine of a lorry was running, but there was no sign of movement in the German camp. A sentry squatted a couple of hundred metres away, rubbing his eyes and yawning.

He would be awake, Yael thought. She imagined him waking alone in his bed and rising and wondering where she was. The pain in her heart was so intense she thought it would break. She hungered for him. For the small meaningless rituals that made up their days. *Oi* Aleksei, she thought, what am I to do? Where am I to go?

She felt suddenly nauseous. She bent down and vomited on the pine needles and thin grass. What little there was in her stomach came up with the bitter taste of bile. Worried the sound of her retching would attract the sentry, she turned and shuffled back into the woods, wiping her mouth with the cuff of her sleeve. Seeking out her hideaway in the thorn bushes, she lay down and rested some more.

The sun rose. It was a warm day, even in the shade of the forest. The Germans did not venture into the woods and Yael felt unable to move. The nausea left her after a while, but still she could not find the will to lift her body from the soft earth. She did not know what to do, or where to go. Later in the afternoon a deer poked around close to her. She withdrew herself frightened. When it had gone, she pulled herself out of the thicket and wandered once more down towards the edge of the woods to look out over the farm. The Germans had not moved, and showed little sign of doing so. Another soldier was on duty, pacing smartly across the field, working his way up towards the forest rim, south of where she stood. Other soldiers were lounging on the grass outside the farmhouse, cleaning rifles and boots, laughing and joking quietly among themselves. There was no sign of Aleksei.

It was late when she started looking for food. There was little available in the close proximity of the farmhouse. She knew where to find fruit bushes, but most of the ripe fruit had been picked, and so she was forced to pick green berries, which were so sour she preferred not to try them despite her growing hunger. She found the same thicket to sleep in that night, but huddling herself away in the tangle of thorny tendrils, she could not sleep. She lay far into the night, caught between fear and loneliness in the eternity of darkness.

The next day she felt sick again. She worried she had caught some fever, and thought of Rivka, dying in the woods. Further south there were more fruit bushes, wild berries and possibly mushrooms, Velvet Shank or Wood Blewits, and she went in search of these. She walked for a couple of hours, not wanting to go too far from the farm, nor to get lost, but she could find little food. That evening she felt faint. She sat at the base of a tree, her head in her hands, her stomach empty.

The third day she began to panic. There was little food available in the immediate vicinity and she was forced to explore further afield. She got lost in the afternoon and sat weeping for an hour. When the sun began to set, she regained her sense of direction and began making her way back through the forest towards Aleksei's house, but she had gone too far, and weariness overcame her.

She found it hard to concentrate and stumbled on the roots of trees. She fell once, banging her arm, chafing the skin. She cried for a while again, before pulling herself up and forcing herself on. The forest grew dimmer as she walked. At first she thought it was evening drawing in rapidly, but shaking her head and resting against the trunk of an old oak, she found it brightened a little. She slumped to the floor and held her head between her hands. Her head swirled, and the nausea returned. Before she knew it there was total blackness.

★　★　★

Before she awoke she was aware of the movements around her. She lay still, drifting slowly out from the heart of darkness, her eyes pressed tightly closed. The voices and footsteps mingled with her dreams and for a while she struggled to separate them. The last image to flicker across her brain was of a stork. It sank down from the sky, its wings outstretched and landed over her, one red leg planted pole-like on either side of her. Raising its wings it clattered its beak, nodding its head up and down.

Opening her eyes she found a figure standing over her, blocking out the last of the sun's rays.

23

The figure standing above her so frightened Yael, she wished she could faint again; that the darkness of unconsciousness would envelop her. She did not though. The light cut through the canopy of leaves with the last piercing fierceness of a July sunset, silhouetting the man.

Seeing her eyelids flicker, he bent down so that his face was close to hers, and she felt his breath on her cheek. It smelt of tobacco fumes and something sharper, which she did not recognise at first, but afterwards realised was alcohol.

'Anna,' he called, turning his head away.

Yael opened her eyes a crack and caught a glimpse of his turned face. A strong jaw and prominent nose made his face seem determined. When he turned back, she squeezed her eyes closed again. He obviously noted this, for he laughed, a low, ironic chuckle.

'Anna,' he called again, 'the forest spirit has awoken.'

He stood up and turned away. She heard the catch of a match, its sudden flaring and then a moment later caught the scent of tobacco. He moved away, but was replaced immediately by a young woman with short dark hair. Anna squatted down beside Yael and took one of her wrists in her hand, expertly placing fingers on her pulse, feeling for a minute, before laying it back on the earth carefully. She opened Yael's eye with a firm, expert touch. For a few seconds she examined her, then grinned, holding her eyelid open so that Yael was forced to look directly at her.

'Hello,' she said. Her grin was a little lop-sided, but it was frank and open and Yael could not help but smile back.

'There,' Anna called over her shoulder to the retreating male figure, 'she's smiling! I told you she wasn't a *dybbuk*.'

'We'll see,' the voice drifted back.

★ ★ ★

Anna helped Yael to sit up. It was only when she was upright, her back rested against the trunk of a thick old birch, that she realised she was not where she last recalled being.

'Where are we?' she said. Her voice was thin, almost inaudible.

'Where are we?' Anna repeated. She had a metal canteen; she unscrewed the lid and passed it to Yael.

'God only knows. The middle of the forest. A hole in the woods. Ask Maksim.'

Yael took the canteen and brought it to her lips. Her hand was unsteady. She shook so much Anna reached out and steadied it.

'You're weak,' Anna said. 'When was the last time you ate?'

Yael shrugged. She was disorientated. The liquid was cool on her tongue, but she had trouble swallowing and choked when she tried to reply.

'It's okay,' Anna said, 'you don't need to speak. I'll get you something to eat in a bit. Some soup. Something light, you need to be careful. It can be too much, you know, eating a lot when you've been without. There was this guy we found last year, hadn't eaten much in weeks before he joined us. Stuffed himself. Couldn't stop. Stole food from the store while the others were sleeping. It killed him. His body couldn't take it.'

Anna spoke quickly, the words tumbling out in a curious accent. She used the American word 'guy', which made her sound as though she had watched too many films. Perhaps seeing her effect on Yael, she laughed.

'Don't mind me,' she said, sitting back on her heels, 'I always talk too much. Maksim says I'm his first line of defence, if the

Germans come, he'll pick me up under his arm and machine-gun them with words!'

She laughed again, openly, heartily, and Yael found she could not restrain her own smile, despite feeling wretched. As Anna stood up, Yael glanced past her to the camp spread out in the trees. At its heart a small fire burned, and around it a large group of people stood or squatted. Blankets and sheets of canvas were tied between branches forming rudimentary shelters. Some of the people were armed, an array of weapons: a woman had a pistol tucked in her belt, as also, Yael now noticed, did Anna, two men had rifles slung in the crooks of their arms, and a machine gun of the type the Germans used stood on a tripod at the edge of the camp. These were not just young men and women though, there were old women and men shuffling around and children squatting by the fire, poking sticks into the flames. Yael was astounded.

'Who are these people?' she croaked.

'Who, these?' Anna said, turning to survey the figures as though she had not really thought about them before. 'They're family! Our big family! I'll be right back.'

Anna walked across to the fire; Yael felt she had not meant her words literally, though looking around it could indeed have been a large tribe. A ragged family come out to camp in the woods. Jewish gypsies. It reminded her of a Sukkoth celebration from her childhood, when they had pitched a tent in the field of her aunt's home. The whole family had lived in the tents for the week. It had been clear autumn weather, cold and damp in the morning, but clearing to bright dry days. The children made fires and played, and in the evenings listened to the bible stories, though none of the family were particularly religious. Yael loved to crouch by the bonfire in the evenings, as the first stars pierced the inky sky, and gaze deep into the flames, imagining she was an Israelite escaped from Egypt, from slavery.

The man who had been stood over her, Maksim, was standing at the edge of the camp, in conversation. Anna crossed over to him and he bent his head to listen to her, then nodded and glanced across at Yael. Yael felt her cheeks flush as his eyes rested on her for a couple of seconds. But then he turned away, and Anna left him to his discussion with the young partisan wearing a black cap on the back of his head.

Anna brought her soup. A young boy had wandered away from the family group and edged closer to her, his eyes wide.

'Aunt,' he whispered, 'is she dead?'

'Does she look dead?' Anna shot back across her shoulder. The young boy regarded

Yael, chewing his nails. He did not seem sure. He came no closer, but squatted down to watch as Anna spooned the soup carefully into Yael's mouth.

'We didn't know if you would make it,' Anna explained as she offered the thin broth, which was little more than water flavoured with vegetables. 'We had been on a raid, a small town twenty odd kilometres north of here. We found you as we were coming back. The boys thought you should be left, but Max was having none of it. 'We can't feed any more,' they said. 'She dies then she won't be eating,' Max figures, 'she lives, you never know, she could help us.'' Anna grinned. 'Where you from?'

'From?' Yael coughed, as she struggled to sip the soup slowly from Anna's spoon. 'I was from Selo.'

'Selo? They killed the Jews there years ago.'

Yael did not know how to respond. The spoon had paused some centimetres from her mouth as Anna waited for a response. Yael felt exhausted. She longed for Aleksei. For the quiet certainty of the life they had lived in the confines of that little home.

'I've been hiding,' she managed.

'You've been with a partisan group? You've been in the woods for two years? Who have you been with?'

165

Yael shook her head. 'No, I've been sheltered. The Germans came. I had to run.'

Anna nodded. The faint outlines of her story seemed to suffice. Anna spooned the last of the soup into her mouth.

'Do you think you can walk? We can move you in closer to the fire.'

An elderly woman had detached herself from the huddled group around the small fire. She came over and took the shoulder of the boy, who was squatted amongst the leaves. Pulling the boy up, she turned to go, but then stopped, her eyes caught by Yael's.

'*Ei, ei ei!*' she cried quietly.

She released the child's shoulder and stepped closer to Yael. Her face was wrinkled, the skin dark, dirty and creased like old leather. Her eyes sparkled though. She bent down, pushing her face closer to Yael. Yael drew back from her, a little afraid. The woman's hand reached out and touched her face. Her breath hissed like a burst pipe.

'Ei, so,' she muttered.

'What is it?' Anna asked the elderly woman, respectfully. 'What do you see?'

'She's *trógedik* my dear,' the woman hissed. Then stepping back and straightening up, her eyes not leaving Yael's, 'She's with child.'

24

Yael trembled. The old woman looked at her for a few moments longer, smiled at her pitifully, revealing a mouth almost totally devoid of teeth, then turned away, her hand on the shoulder of the young boy. Anna's eyes widened.

'Pregnant?'

Yael struggled to find her voice but could not. Could not find words that might arrest the free-fall of her emotions. Instinctively her hand flew to her belly.

'Is it possible?' Anna asked. 'Where is your husband? He was with you?'

The sun dipped and the air was suddenly sharp with the cool breath of evening. Through the canopy of yellowing leaves, Yael could see the sky speckled like the belly of a trout. Her lips moved, but no sound emerged.

'She is never wrong, old Fayga. She has the ability to see.' Anna bent closer and rested the palm of her hand gently next to Yael's. Yael felt the soft pressure of its weight. Anna touched her fingers. 'You didn't know?'

Yael shook her head. She could not believe the old woman's words, and yet suddenly she knew, she felt in the very core of her being, the truth of it. That it was so. That she was bearing a child. That she was bearing his child. That, at the age of sixteen, in the midst of war, in the midst of horror, this time of madness and death, she was to give birth to the child of a mute.

'Where is the father?' Anna asked again, her voice soft with concern.

All Yael could do was to wave her hand in the vague direction she felt Aleksei's farm was. She could still find no words that might encompass her shock, that might make normal a world set once more upon its head.

'Is he alive?'

Yael shook her head, signifying only her inability to comprehend, but Anna let out a low moan and clenched her fingers tight, squeezing them so that they hurt. Her eyes pressed closed and a tear fell down her cheek.

'It's not that . . . ' Yael began, but Anna stopped her, with a finger laid gently upon her lips.

'It's okay,' she whispered. She leant forward and hugged her tight, so that Yael could smell the pleasant fragrance of her body, the scent of tobacco on her hair and the faint mustiness of her clothes. Releasing her, Anna got up.

'You stay there, don't move!' she said. 'I'll

get a couple of the boys to move you closer towards the fire.'

'There's no need to worry,' Yael stammered, 'I'm feeling much better.' But already Anna had turned away and was heading back across the forest floor to the fire and the huddled groups.

'Oh Aleksei!' Yael breathed, pressing her eyes tightly closed. She could not conceive of a child in her womb. It made no sense — but the thought of it, the thought of life stirring inside her — the picture of a baby cradled in her arms as she stood beside Aleksei, filled her with an inexpressibly sharp pain that threatened to overwhelm her again. She had to get back to him. That was the one thought that circled round and round her head, I must get back to the farm. I must.

'How are you feeling?'

Yael opened her eyes, startled at the male voice so close to her. Maksim was kneeling in the leaves by her side. His face was sober with concern. He seemed to wish to reach out and touch her, but restrained himself.

'I'm fine,' Yael said.

'The old one says you're pregnant.'

Yael nodded, her hand over her belly, as if, perhaps, protecting the seed implanted in her womb.

'She could be wrong,' Maksim said,

rocking back on the heels of his leather boots. But he said it without conviction, as if he too believed in the old woman's capacity to see what others could not. The concept that she might not be pregnant ricocheted around Yael's heart, startling her once more, at how ready she had been to believe, and how much, despite everything, she wanted it to be, wanted to know that she was not alone, would never be alone, that Aleksei was not distant but now forever a part of her. That something had been born of that peace and happiness.

Maksim stood up. He brushed the dirt and leaves from his trousers and looked back over his shoulder at the two young men who were approaching with a blanket.

'Nu, va,' he said, slowly, almost sadly, Yael thought. 'May God bless you.'

'Thank you,' she said.

'Come on then!'

The two boys were little older than Yael. They were muscular, not large, but strong, with tough-looking faces that were split with grins. They spread the blanket on the ground and carefully lifted Yael onto it.

'I can walk,' Yael protested.

'Maybe,' one of the boys said, 'but Anna will give my ear a tongue-lashing if we let you.'

Between the two of them they lifted the corners of the blanket onto their shoulders, forming a stretcher, and hauled her across to the fire. Yael felt the eyes on her as she approached the large crowd of people that milled around. Old morose men sat slumped before makeshift shelters, women stood talking, quietening as she passed, clicking their tongues and shaking their heads. Small children ran about, scattering leaves.

The boys slowly lowered the blanket onto the ground by a shelter made from birch and roofed with branches of fir, the needles of which were brown now and shrinking back, leaving gaps through which Yael could see the last remaining light of day.

* * *

The camp was split into two groups: there were the partisans, mainly young men and women, and then there were the elderly, the sick and the children. It consisted of perhaps fifteen young people, Yael counted, most of a similar age to her, though Maksim was probably in his late twenties and there were two men who were in their thirties, one of whom was slightly retarded, but, Anna assured her, a brave soldier and almost invisible when he wished to be.

171

Maksim drilled the partisans daily and held frequent meetings with scouts who constantly reported back to the camp concerning the whereabouts of the Germans. Occasionally small groups disappeared into the woods. Sometimes they would be gone for days at a time. When they returned, they would empty out bags of food onto a blanket and Anna would divide it up and log it to ensure a proper record was kept so no one could steal any, or to prevent the risk that anybody should be favoured, or be seen to be favoured more than others.

The older women took care of the cooking and Yael was amazed at what they managed to produce from the meagre supplies brought back by the partisans and from the herbs and fruits of the forest and game trapped by the men. As the autumn drew on, they enjoyed a diet of rabbit, mushrooms and wild vegetables. Yael's health returned. Within days she was on her feet, feeling vigour return to her muscles. She did not like being counted among the sick and elderly.

'What can I do,' she asked Anna, 'to be useful?'

'You can get well,' Anna said. 'You will be no good to anybody should you get sick.'

Anna was a pretty young girl. She wore a fur coat decorated with a leopard-skin

172

pattern. 'Fake,' she told Yael. 'It used to belong to my grandmother who had bourgeois pretensions, but was never anything more than a provincial shopkeeper's wife and not a very successful one at that, no matter how hard she pushed my poor grandfather.' Anna's hair was dark and shoulder-length. She was quite short, shorter even than Yael, but her ebullient personality made up for it.

'Maksim laughs at me for this,' Anna chuckled, fingering the coat. 'He says I am no better than grandma, dreaming of marrying a rich capitalist, like in the American films.'

They glanced across the forest floor to where Maksim was sitting with a group of three young men who had returned from scouting the north. He was seated leaning back against the trunk of a thick birch, his military jacket flapping open, cigarette smoking in the corner of his mouth. Maksim carried a quiet authority. He seemed to be respected by everyone in the camp, particularly the elderly, who he took the time to talk to each evening. The small boys would salute him and he would salute them back. The response never failed to suffuse the boys' faces with a glow of pride.

'He looks sad,' Yael said to Anna.

'Maksim?'

'I mean,' Yael clarified, 'he seems so quiet

and controlled, as though he is somewhere else, or wishes he was. But I suppose that's understandable. We all do.' She looked away, watching the young children chase each other round the fire.

'He is a private man,' Anna said. 'He does not speak much of himself.'

'Where is he from?'

'From Russia. Nobody knows quite where. There are stories . . . ' she paused, glancing across at Maksim. 'That he barely escaped Stalin's purges. He is a hero but he is not a communist.'

Yael looked at Anna, noting the tone of respect, of affection, but Anna caught the glance and laughed. 'You think I have feelings for Maksim?' she said. 'Don't worry, I'm not a romantic, and I'm not in love with Maksim. He is a great leader though. A brave man. But that is it.'

She paused, then reached out and touched Yael's hand. 'And your husband? You miss him? What was his name?'

'Aleksei,' she answered truthfully.

'What happened?'

But Yael shook her head. She realised she was wilfully allowing Anna to continue with the misconception that she had been married and that her husband was dead, but she could not begin, did not want to begin to explain her story to the young Jewish girl.

Later that evening when Anna had left her Yael considered her next move. Now she was feeling so much healthier, she longed to start back towards the farm to see if the Germans had moved on, to see whether it was safe to return. She imagined running down the slope to the farmhouse, Aleksei opening the door and her falling into his arms. She imagined the look on his face, late in the evening, as they lay in bed when she would tell him she was pregnant. That she was bearing their child. She fell asleep that night planning the journey back through the woods.

25

She woke to the sound of movement. Opening her eyes she could see figures flickering in the faint pre-dawn light. One of the partisans was kicking over the smouldering embers of the fire, while others were pulling down the shelters from the trees. Yael sat up, rubbing her eyes. It was a cold morning. Her bones were stiff and her muscles ached when she moved.

'What is it?' she asked when Anna came by, close to where she had been sleeping.

Anna's pretty face was creased with sleep and concern. 'We have to move,' she said shortly, 'the Nazis are moving closer. There's a platoon just a few miles down the road. Maksim has sent scouts forward to find somewhere safer.' Anna scuttled away, gathering the disparate tribe together, gently shaking awake the elderly, taking care that the store was packed safely and entrusted to a couple of the young partisan soldiers.

By the time the sun had begun to rise they were moving, a long, silent column pushing through the deep undergrowth of the forest. A small group of the partisans stayed back and covered over the evidence of their camp. The traces of the fire were buried and leaves scattered. They took the bloody carcass of a buck that had been killed some days previously and dragged it back and forth, pulling it away in the opposite direction to that taken by the column.

'If the Germans have dogs there is no chance they would not pick up scent of us. Hopefully the smell of the buck will excite them, and it's that trail they will follow,' Anna explained.

They walked for the rest of the morning, making quick progress, despite the thick undergrowth that clotted the heart of the deep forest. As they walked Yael glanced back over her shoulder, as Aleksei's farm became further and further away.

* * *

'The Germans are still afraid of the forests,' another partisan explained to Yael. 'They venture this deep only if they have to. The woods still belong to the partisan groups and they know it.'

By midday they had come to the edge of a lake. The water shimmered, reflecting the dull sunlight. They stopped for a while, the partisans making sure the crowd kept in the shade of the forest, in case planes should pass over.

The lake was in the hollow of a valley. The hills rose around it steeply, heavily wooded. A bird cried. The children shuffled and moaned. The quietness was profound. A large shape skimmed the tops of the trees and swooped down to the side of the lake. The stork settled in the shallows, the water rippling out from its thin legs. It stood motionless as Yael gazed down at it. Its head turned and it seemed to stare up the grass bank to where she was seated. Yael shivered.

A young partisan rose from the group and cocked his rifle. Yael glanced up, as he raised the gun to his shoulder.

'No!'

Maksim stood. He reached out and pushed down the barrel of the rifle. The young partisan frowned.

'The Germans are a long way off now, they will not hear.'

'It's not that,' Maksim explained. 'There's no purpose in killing the stork, it's *treyf*. Forbidden.'

The young partisan laughed. '*Treyf!* And pigs are acceptable?'

Maksim shook his head. He turned away and pulling out a packet of cigarettes from his pocket extracted one. He took his time lighting it. The smoke dissipated slowly in the clear still air.

'The stork is a *tsádik*,' Maksim said seriously. 'In Hebrew its name is *Chasidah*, deriving from the word *chesed* meaning kindness.'

He paused again to take another drag of his cigarette. Yael gazed up at him. His voice was intense, impassioned, and his eyes glittered with energy, though every movement of his body seemed slow and considered, as if he fought to control the vigour of his being.

'If it is such a *tsádik*, then why is it forbidden to eat it?' another of the partisans asked. 'If its essence is clean and good, surely it should be good to eat?'

'That I don't know,' Maksim said, 'but Rashi claimed its name came from the fact that it was kind to its neighbours. It's common knowledge that the stork is the most caring of birds with its young.'

'Listen to him,' one of the older partisans laughed, 'our very own forest *rebbe*!' But the laughter was kind, and even Maksim himself smiled.

★ ★ ★

Later, Maksim stood by the lake's edge, smoking another cigarette. Seeing him there on his own, Yael wandered down to join him.

'Anna was telling me about you,' she said, eying him.

He glanced sideways at her, but said nothing.

'There wasn't much she could tell,' Yael conceded, seeing his look. 'She said you were a very private person.'

'Anna talks too much,' he said, but not unkindly. 'If I told her anything the whole world would know within a few minutes.'

He tossed the cigarette down in the shallows of the water and for a few moments watched as it floated on the surface, its tip sizzling. 'And you . . . ' he paused and turned to look at her fully. She looked down at her feet. 'Little Anna does not seem to have found out too much about you either.'

Yael turned towards the water. The sunlight danced lightly across its silky surface. Maksim seemed about to say something else. His lips opened, but then he seemed to think better of it. He ran his hand through his hair and for moments they stood in silence on the edge of the lake, listening to the sound of the water's gentle lapping, to the murmur of voices from behind them in the forest.

'Do you think we will get through this?' Yael asked, glancing up into his dark features.

He nodded. 'Yes,' he said simply. 'We will.'

He reached out and touched her hair. 'We will.'

* * *

They continued walking in the afternoon, working their way back into the forest. At one point they had to traverse a field. Scouts went out ahead and positioned themselves in various places, then the group split up and hurried across the field in twos and threes, keeping low, trying to remain inconspicuous.

By evening they had marched about ten miles east, working their way closer to the Russian border. All the time Yael was aware they were heading further and further away from Aleksei's farm. When they stopped that evening they began erecting their shelters among the low-slung branches of the trees so they were hidden on all sides by brambles and deep grass. Yael stood at the edge of the camp and gazed back through the trees the way they had come.

Rarely did Yael pray, beyond the ritual words offered occasionally on special feasts and holidays, it was not a custom she had been brought up with, but as she stood facing the setting sun, squinting slightly, she asked that God might allow her to make the journey back, that she might find him once again, and the peace that they had enjoyed might be restored. Placing her hand on her belly she muttered, 'For the child. For our child.' But this did not stop her sense of the foolishness of it. That in the midst of war, as all around the slaughter continued, God should care about the fate of her love. She imagined her prayer as a small flicker of light rising in the late afternoon air, dissolving in the coppery reds, the violet shadows and the darkening blues of the sky. 'A still small voice,' she murmured to herself, remembering the words of her father. 'It was not in the thunder nor the lightening, nor in the strong wind, but in the still small voice that God was.'

When she turned back, she noticed Maksim too was stood on the edge of the camp, smoking a cigarette, gazing out through the trees, and she wondered if he was thinking of a love left miles away.

★ ★ ★

In the partisan unit everybody had their role, even the elders. Some were charged with the task of collecting firewood, keeping the fire burning, some foraged for berries and mushrooms and other edible roots. Others looked after the children, cooked. Some cleaned weapons. There was a tailor who mended clothes and a shoemaker who did his best to keep the unit well shod. Anna was in charge of arranging the domestic duties, whilst Maksim was in overall command of the small partisan unit, and of the soldiers. That night Anna asked Yael to help the women with the children.

There were seven children with the group, ranging in age from four to ten. Esther was the only girl. She was seven years old and wore a red ribbon which was threadbare and greasy from her unwashed hair, but which she insisted on keeping, and treasured, Yael discovered, as if it was the finest silk. While the boys romped, fighting imaginary battles with German troops, Yael sat with Esther in the gathering gloom and combed and plaited the young girl's hair.

'Tell me a story,' Esther demanded, leaning back against Yael.

For some moments Yael hesitated, trying to think of something that would amuse the girl. She told her then about the great grand-mother of the *grafas Tiskevicius*.

'When I was younger, before the war, the school I went to was small. It was held in the house of the *grafas Tiskevicius*. Sometimes the old man would come in and interrupt our lessons. He would tell the story about his great-grandmother.'

'Is it a love story?' The girl asked.

'Yes,' Yael smiled. 'It's a love story.'

Esther nodded, satisfied, and leaned back against her.

'Old man Tiskevicius' great-grandfather was a soldier in Napoleon's army. He was badly injured in the fighting in Russia and barely made it back as far as Selo before falling ill. He had a fever.'

She stroked the girl's hair and gazed out into the growing darkness. In her mind's eye she could see the old man stood by the window of the schoolroom, carefully stuffing his pipe. He smoked an English pipe, the type Sherlock Holmes would smoke in the comic strips.

'He was in the barn. The rest of the soldiers had left, beating their retreat back to France, but he could go no further. His leg was shot to bits. He was burning with fever and hallucinating.

'The men in the village got together and drew lots as to who was going to shoot him.'

'Shoot him? Why?' Esther looked up at her.

'Well, there was a lot of bad feeling about the French army; all the villages they had burned, the food they had stolen. But anyway, none of them wanted to do it, so they figured if they left him he would die anyway. What they didn't know was that a young girl

— the *grafas'* great-grandmother — was secretly looking after the young soldier. She was a beauty and strong-headed too. A vixen, the *grafas* called her. She would creep out at night and bathe his wounds and lay a cool wet cloth across his forehead and take him in her arms and feed him broth.'

'How did he know all this?' Esther asked.

'She was still alive when the *grafas* was young. She told the story to him herself.'

Yael had never questioned the story at school. She listened to the old man raptly as the other children dozed or flicked things at each other.

'After a week the men went into the barn and found him sitting there, on the top of a haystack smoking a cigarette. There was a commotion. The soldier spoke no Polish and only a few words of German, but not enough to communicate. It was clear from the state of him and from the empty bowl the villagers found at his feet that somebody had been looking after him.

'The *grafas'* great-grandmother stood forward, brazen as you like and confessed it had been her that had been feeding and caring for the soldier. Her father picked up a shovel and was advancing on the young girl, but the soldier picked himself up and threw himself between them. He rolled up his sleeves and

185

made it clear that should her father want to fight, he was ready for it.

'The villagers put their heads together for a while and scratched their beards, but there was nothing much they could do about it, so they let him be.'

'Did they get married?'

'Yes, of course. He was a simple man. He never learned more than a handful of Polish words as long as he lived and the *grafas'* great-grandmother never learned any French. As far as he could tell they were never able to talk to each other, but they were married for a good sixty years.'

After she had finished, Esther was silent for some time. 'I don't understand,' she said finally, her voice laced with irritation. 'How could they be married and not speak to each other?'

'I don't know,' Yael said quietly. 'The *grafas* never explained.'

'Perhaps they spoke Yiddish,' Esther suggested.

'No,' Yael replied, 'they didn't speak Yiddish.'

'Then it's a stupid story.'

The *grafas'* great-grandparents' grave was at the back of the churchyard, sheltered from the summer sun by the far-flung bough of an old yew. Yael had gone to see it once and sat before the weathered stone and thought about the story.

'Can you marry someone if you can't speak to them?' She had asked her father later.

'The question is can you speak to somebody if you've married them?' Her father threw back at her, leaning over the shoe he was repairing, tacks sticking from his mouth, a small hammer tapping them into the sole with light precision.

★ ★ ★

'Are you married?' the girl asked her later.

Yael hesitated before she answered. 'Yes,' she said.

'You don't sound very sure.'

'I'm not sure where he is,' Yael said softly. 'My husband.'

'Is he dead?'

'I don't know.'

'Do you miss him?'

Yael gazed up through the roof of the trees. 'Yes,' she said. 'Terribly.'

26

Autumn came slowly: the scent of decay, the tips of leaves curling and sudden blusters that sent them twirling to the earth. At night it grew colder sleeping in the woods. The partisans crept together, sharing the heat between their huddled bodies. Yael slept with the young girl wrapped tight around her. Esther slept soundly every night and Yael envied her this ability to shut off. Whenever Yael shut her eyes, she was troubled by visions. Often she preferred just to lie there, gazing out across the silent camp; the dull embers of the fire, shrouded to keep its light from the Germans, the knots of supine bodies, the moon shadows, or wisps of fog that hung between the trees; Maksim constantly awake, pacing back and forth, cigarette burning between his fingers.

More and more often the scouts were coming back with reports of German divisions moving into the neighbouring areas. There was talk of Soviet advances, that the Germans were retreating, but then others speculated of another German push and that it was the Russians who were beaten not the Nazis.

There was also talk of other partisan groups operating in the area. As Yael squatted by the fire one evening, listening to the conversation around her, her ears picked out a name and the hairs on the back of her neck stood on end.

'Josef Alterman?' she asked. She stood up suddenly, her heart beating rapidly.

The scout, a nineteen-year-old boy called Yakov Kopel, who had a handsome face, but both of his front teeth missing, turned to Yael. He shrugged.

'I don't know about that,' he said. 'They call him *Volk*. The Wolf.'

'Describe him,' Yael begged. 'Please?'

Yakov looked at her, a little irritated. He flicked a glance at Maksim, to whom he had been talking, but Maksim nodded for him to do as Yael asked. He described the partisan leader he had been telling Maksim about. Yael nodded, listening intently. She was sure it was her brother.

'Where are they?' Yael asked.

'He commands a small unit, they're highly mobile; a quick raid here or there and then they're moving on. They have a girl with them, from what I've heard, but apart from that it's only The Wolf and five other men.

They're local Jews as far as I know, they know the area well, but they're backed by the Soviets, they're all well equipped.'

That night, when finally she fell asleep, she dreamt of him. He was seated on the back of his horse, riding through the forest, neat in his Red Army uniform.

The idea that he might be close filled Yael with joy. She felt a renewed energy in her step, a vitality she had not felt for months. In the hours when she was not helping out, doing her chores, she begged Anna to teach her how to shoot.

The feel of the smooth butt of the rifle snuggled against her cheek, the hard recoil against her shoulder, the cold metal beneath her finger, the scent of gunpowder excited her. She found she was a good shot. She had a steady hand and a good eye. After a couple of days, her shoulder ached and, peeling back her shirt, she found the skin bruised blue and yellow. She probed the tender flesh with the tips of her fingers, and relished the pain. It was a badge, a mark of a new courage she felt welling up from the core of her being.

When Maksim praised her shot to Anna, Yael couldn't help but feel proud. Giving Esther back to the other women, Yael spent as many of her nights as possible volunteering for sentry duty, preferring to wander the quiet edge of the camp, eyes stretched against the darkness, the weight of the rifle looped across her shoulder, to lying sleepless among the other women.

As she sensed the tiny child budding in her belly, no bigger than a kidney bean, perversely she felt a growing desire to kill. To protect. The strength of the feeling scared her.

'When you go out on a raid,' she said to Anna, as they did sentry duty together, 'do you feel scared?'

'Yes,' Anna said.

They were sitting on a log thirty metres away from the camp and through the thick undergrowth and the tree trunks it was almost invisible.

'Have you ever killed anybody?'

'I don't know,' Anna answered. 'There have been times when we have been caught in a fight and there has been shooting, but it's hard to tell.'

'Anna,' Yael breathed, flushing as she spoke, 'sometimes when I have the rifle in my hands I have such a desire to kill. Do you think that is wrong?'

Anna flicked a glance at her. Yael's face was scarcely visible in the darkness. Anna snaked her arm around her shoulder and squeezed her.

'We all long to kill them,' she whispered. 'How could we not? Do you remember the story of Deborah? We are Deborah's children, Yael. Deborah and Jael.'

Yael recalled the story of Jael, of the tent peg nailed through the commander's temple as he rested in her care. As a child she struggled to understand that level of violence. But now there was a depth of comprehension she could never have wished for.

★ ★ ★

Maksim was reluctant when Anna suggested it. He had just shaved down by the stream and his face glowed. He shook his head and cast a glance across Anna's shoulder at Yael who stood back a few paces, the rifle cradled in her hands. He clicked his tongue and turned away, gazing off into the empty distance for some moments before turning, his forehead creased.

'There are many ways of helping,' he said. 'Many ways to serve the cause. They are all important. Where would the children be if there was no one to care for them? Where would we be if there was no one to cook? The old ones . . . ' His voice trailed off as he saw the look on Anna's face. 'Don't look at me like that, Anna.'

'It's like that again is it, Maksim?' she said frostily, as if picking up the thread of an old argument.

Maksim ran a hand through his hair. He looked over at Yael, as if in appeal to her, but seeing the look on her face, he sighed.

'Now you're ganging up on me!'

'Oh, you had better believe it,' Anna said. 'And you won't stand a chance against us. Try her. One raid. Let her come.'

'It's madness!'

'This war is mad! What is the point in sanity?'

'She's pregnant!'

'Yakov has his two front teeth missing.'

'What has that to do with anything?'

'Exactly!'

Maksim moaned. He shook his head though and turned and walked away up from the bank of the river to the camp. Yael felt it like a stab in the heart. She had to do something. To feel useful. Anything to pass the time until she was back with Aleksei.

★　★　★

The railway line was a little over eight miles away. The traffic on it was regular, supplies heading east after the German troops, and west, stuffed with the broken bodies and the dead. They set off late one evening at the beginning of November. It had grown cold, but it was wet still and there was the probability of fog by early morning. Yael now had the slightest of bumps and she lightly cradled it as they walked.

Anna touched Yael's hand as they left the camp. Yael turned and grinned. Her heart pounded and her muscles were tight with nerves. Maksim was at the head of the line, Yakov and Meyer Feldman, a medical student with a thin, cadaverous skull, followed behind him. Yael did not know what Anna had said to change Maksim's mind; she strongly suspected she had simply talked him into submission. He looked tired and had looked at her wearily when she joined the small party at the edge of the camp. He said nothing though, simply issued orders, checked ammunition and coordinates, and then led the way off between the trees.

They walked until four o'clock in the morning. The ground was wet and muddy and often Yael found herself stumbling in the darkness. She was breathless, and her side ached. The rifle strap had rubbed her shoulder raw. Just after one o'clock, they had almost walked into a German division. Silently, slowly, they had to work their way back through the trees, losing half an hour as

194

they tacked widely around.

'Regretting coming?' Yakov whispered. It was so dark Yael could make out only the faint outline of his face.

'Shut up, Yakov,' Anna said. She laid a hand on Yael's shoulder. Yael pressed her hand.

'I'm okay,' she whispered.

There were German sentries at regular points along the line. The scouts had left a concealed trail, to a point where, the previous evening, there had been clear access to the railway, out of sight of any sentry position. This they followed, crawling the last few hundred metres on their bellies, silently, afraid of alerting the dogs. Yael's heart knocked against her ribs. Her whole body was trembling and her teeth chatted so much Yakov turned back and hissed a warning at her. She clenched them so tight against each other her jaw ached. Despite the raw wetness of the night, the mud that smeared her and the dampness of the ground which soaked through her fatigues, Yael was drenched with sweat by the time they huddled in a low gully within sight of the railway line.

Maksim indicated for Yael to move out wide on the flank to help cover the position, Meyer moved out in the other direction. Maksim and Yakov slid forward on their bellies, up the shale slope towards the lines.

Even in the dim moonless night they looked painfully conspicuous to Yael who crouched, shivering, thirty metres further along the line shaded by some thick brush.

The railway line curved around a slow bend, descending a hill, the line cut in tight against rocks on the far side. On the near side the forest was thick and brush grew up to the edge of the gully that ran alongside the track. Peering down the hill, Yael watched for signs of movement. The line was clear. Dark. Silent.

Maksim and Yakov were bent over the train track. Their bodies dark against the pale stone bank. Yael counted slowly to a hundred. She turned, but they were still there working away on the line. The German sentry was standing in the middle of the track when her eyes focused back on the dark slope. He stood with his back to them, fifty metres away, at the slow curve in the line. Yael's heart leapt and the blood drained from her face.

In what seemed like slow motion to her, she raised the rifle and sighted him. He stood in the centre of the lines, a dog on a leash quietly beside him. A match flared, illuminating for a moment his clean-shaven face, as he turned to hide the flame from the breeze. She counted slowly backwards from ten, steadying her nerves, measuring her breaths, feeling the cold metal of the trigger beneath her finger, knowing intimately now the exact pressure that would be required, ready for the steady squeeze, tightening her grip for the recoil, keeping the barrel down. She could hit him from this distance, she knew. She could hit him square in the forehead if he turned a little more.

The light of his cigarette danced as he raised it to his lips, drew in the smoke and then let it drop to his side. Her muscles had relaxed. She felt like an athlete, ready, primed, awaiting the signal. Her glance flicked back and forth, monitoring the situation. The dog looked up. A slight breeze blew up the hill, bringing on it the scent of the tobacco. From behind her she heard the scrape of gravel. The dog flinched. The man reached down and stroked its head. The dog stood up, its neck straining, ears cocked. He flicked away the cigarette. It bounced off the steel line, sparks dancing in the darkness. Yael closed her left eye. Felt the muscles tighten around her right, as she sighted him once again. She eased the rifle in her hands, felt its weight comfortable in her grip. Pressed lightly against the trigger, felt its slight stiffness. He turned then, muttering something to the dog and paced down the line. Yael's eye narrowed. His back was broad. An easy target. She felt her body float, weightless for one moment. Felt she was one with the rifle. Felt the power in her finger. She breathed out. A long slow exhalation. She lowered the gun. Placed it carefully on the ground beside her and wiped the perspiration from her palms. One swift blow. She thought of Jael and was disappointed.

'Let's move!'

Yakov was beside her, pulling at her sleeve. They hurried back through the undergrowth.

'It's on a three-minute timer,' Maksim said, breathless as they pushed through the thick brush, the supple, thin branches of the birch snapping against their faces.

The force of the blast knocked Yael off her feet. Lying in the mud, she felt its heat race across her. The night was suddenly bright. Above her the tree was burning. Getting to her feet she raced alongside Maksim. He turned and she saw he was grinning. He reached out and grasped her hand.

'You okay?' he mouthed.

'Yes,' she stammered. 'Yes.'

27

By the fire, warming her hands, the partisan group milling around her noisily, Yael found she was shaking. It was not that she had feared being killed, she thought, as she crouched down watching the uncontrollable dance of her fingers before her, it was fear that she was able to kill. That she should desire it. That she had never felt so powerful, so one with the world, as she had felt with the rifle aimed at the unknowing German soldier.

More than anything then, she wished to be back in the farmhouse with Aleksei. She longed with an aching painfulness for the quietness of his company, the silent sense of him beside her. With her.

'How are you feeling?' Maksim asked, squatting down next to the fire. She glanced up at his face. It was closed, blank, with no evidence of the boisterous joy of the others.

'I'm fine,' she said, pulling her eyes from his fixed gaze.

She felt his fingers on her back, tracing a gentle line down her spine that made her skin tingle.

'You did good,' he whispered.

Yael nodded. She did not look up as he shifted and rose to his feet. He stood for a few moments beside her as if he wished to say something further. He cleared his throat and it reminded her of Aleksei. She picked up a twig and poked it into the flames, watching it flare. He turned and walked away. Yael let out her breath in a long slow exhalation.

Some time later Anna joined her by the fire and talked and talked in a high, excited pitch of which Yael caught barely a word. Maksim had taken up his position again at the edge of the camp, smoking another of his cigarettes. How lonely he looked, she thought, and how sad.

★ ★ ★

By late November the winter had begun to close in. They woke frequently to frosts and the older members of the group and the children had begun to suffer. Late one evening a small group of scouts returned with news that they had discovered an old *zemlyanka*, a hideout in the woods, constructed by some other partisan group which had clearly moved on.

'Can we be sure it's secure?'

'It seems undisturbed. There are no signs the Germans know of its existence.'

The dugout was fifteen miles to the north, deep in the forest close to the border, wild country, where the Germans remained close to the towns and on the roads. Bears, boar and elk roamed the deep forests, along with hungry wolf packs and partisans of every political persuasion.

An icy, slanting rain fell as the partisan group moved through the woods. The elderly found it difficult moving through the thick mud and Maksim worried continually about the wide trail they were leaving, a clear sign post to any German patrols that might pass through. He left a couple of men behind to try to cover over tracks, by dragging branches across the footprints, but all they could hope for really was that the snow might set in soon and cover it all over for a few months.

The dugout was invisible to the unknowing eye. The scouts themselves admitted they had found it by accident chasing a hare for dinner. Its entrance was hidden beneath the thick tangle of branches of a large fallen fir tree and it was necessary to crawl on hands and knees to the narrow hole in the ground. There were murmurs of protest from some of the elderly.

'It's like going down into the grave!'

'Think of it more,' Maksim cajoled them gently, 'as if you were a rabbit going down into its burrow. The snow will set in soon,' he added. 'There is no way we will all survive a winter out in the open.'

The burrow was much larger than the tight entrance suggested. After a few feet it opened out into a passage, which it was possible to walk in, though bent almost double, running down a slight slope for twenty metres. This passage opened out into a large room around the walls of which crude bunks had been erected. The lower bunks were little more than earth mounds, covered with old planks, while the upper ones were constructed from timber cut from the forest. In the centre of the *zemlyanka* was a small wood-burning stove, its long, rusty pipe rising up through the low roof and out into the woods. There were two or three other pipes that provided access to clean air.

Despite its size the dugout was still cramped when the whole company had pressed down into it. It was dry and warm though, and a relief from the driving rain. Here, as in the previous camp, Anna quickly set up an ordered system, allocating responsibilities to several of the partisans, and to the elder people. Almost immediately work began enlarging the structure. While three of the young partisans dug a new room against the back wall, the others formed a chain and carried the loose earth up and out of the dugout. The earth was carried in sheets two miles west and scattered in various places, so there would be no sign of the work close to the hideaway. Wood was also cut at some distance away and worked into the correct lengths and shapes before being brought back to form the struts and braces and lining for the new room.

Yael worked hard with the others, relishing the physical work. As the weeks passed, she began to really feel the swell of her womb. The baby was growing. It developed as the new centre of her gravity, as though this baby growing inside her was the core of her being, the source of her strength and balance. In the evening she lay in her bunk, on her back, stroking the barely perceptible bulge, focusing her energy on it, speaking to it, silently, willing it to be strong.

⋆ ⋆ ⋆

By December the rain had turned to ice, sharp pellets that stung the skin as the wind whipped against the partisans. Whilst most of the group had retreated into the dugout, like animals hibernating for the winter, Yael went out with the partisans. She no longer desired to take the rifle, preferring to act as medic.

She had learned some nursing skills from Meyer, and Anna taught her how to make a splint and to tear up a shirt for bandaging.

They continued to make raids on villages, stationing themselves on each of the main roads and at various points between the houses, alert and ready to run. They would always ask politely first, knocking on the door of the shopkeeper, introducing themselves as partisans struggling for the liberation of Poland. It was evident from their appearance, though, that they were Jews and first visits were rarely met with sympathy. It was only when the mood turned ugly that the rifles appeared. Things always turned politer then. Maksim would be addressed as *Pan* and the shopkeeper and his neighbour would assure them they sympathised with the partisans.

Yael felt a degree of sympathy for the villagers, who would be in trouble whatever their reaction. If the Germans discovered they were feeding Jews they would execute the men in the village. When, during one raid, the shopkeeper abused Maksim, telling him the Germans were right to have dealt with them so harshly, the partisans took him out and stood him against the back wall of his shop and shot him.

Standing by, Yael was horrified. When Maksim turned away from the crumpled body, his eyes caught hers, and she saw the pain in them and a dark, terrible emptiness. He brushed past her, but she caught his arm. For a moment he paused and she heard his heavy breathing. She pressed her forehead against his shoulder, and stroked the rough stubble on his chin. Trying to offer some comfort, no matter how small. The war was leading them all further and further away from themselves.

'You shouldn't come out with us,' he said to her that evening. They were on sentry duty, and walked continually back and forth to keep warm. 'You need to take care of yourself.' He paused, and turning, laid a hand gently on her stomach. Yael felt her heart flutter. She looked away embarrassed.

'My mother is dead, my father is dead. I have no one left. What does it matter what happens now? What is there left?'

'Our children,' he whispered passionately, his face close to hers. 'Our future.'

'What future is possible?' she said urgently, taking hold of his arms, and looking at him in the dim light of the moon. 'They have ripped our world apart. It no longer exists. What can we do when this all finishes? If this ever finishes? We cannot go back to the *shtetl*. It's gone. It's all gone.'

Maksim opened his mouth to answer, but

then after a few moments just shook his head. 'I don't know,' he whispered. 'I don't know how to answer that. All I know is that we must survive. We must not let them win.'

'Exactly!' Yael said, her voice rich with triumph. 'That is all that is left for us. To fight to make sure they do not win. There is no longer any meaning to our lives beyond that.'

Maksim stepped back from her, shaking his head. He took out a cigarette and then offered Yael one. She hesitated a moment, then reached out and took one. She had never smoked a cigarette before and did not even know how to hold it. It felt surprisingly light and insubstantial in her fingers. She imitated the way she had seen Eva holding the cigarette, and placed it delicately between her lips. Maksim, watching her, smiled.

'Your first?'

Yael nodded, but gave him a look that challenged him to make fun of her. He flicked the flint of his lighter and the dancing flame illuminated his face. He held it to the end of her cigarette.

'Inhale gently,' he told her.

She did as he said and got a throat full of the smoke. It stung her, the bitter, acrid taste filling her mouth and making her choke. Taking it out she coughed, then cursed herself for looking a fool. Maksim didn't laugh though. He lit his own and inhaled the smoke deeply, then breathed it out in a long, slow exhalation.

'Will you go back Russia,' Yael asked, 'when all this is finished, if ever it is?'

'Back into Stalin's arms?' he chuckled. 'To them we are the *bezrodnye*. Rootless. However much we may try, however many centuries we may live there, no matter that our writers should enrich their language, our composers their musical tradition, our children's blood feed the dark soil of the fatherland, we shall never belong in their eyes.'

He shrugged and then looked at her. For some moments he held her gaze. She was taken aback by the intimacy of the moment.

'I was arrested before the war,' he said. 'Do you know what my crime was? Translating and publishing the work of decadent writers. I was accused of 'cosmopolitanism' — indifference to the fatherland and to the national tradition and to the national culture.'

He shook his head and looked away. She saw the muscles tighten his jaw. Sensing there was more he was holding back from telling her, she reached out and touched his arm.

'What happened?'

'There was . . . ' he looked at her. 'It doesn't matter.'

'Tell me.'

'Why? What is the good? It does nothing to linger over these things now.'

'Sometimes that's all I feel we can do, hang onto these bitter memories, let them feed our hatred, how else can we go out and do what we did today?'

He hesitated. 'There was a young woman I knew, before the war.'

Yael nodded, but Maksim did not want to carry on.

'I was in love,' was all he would say and shook his head, as if dispelling the thought. A clear image played across Yael's mind of Maksim stepping down from a train and of a woman running forward to greet him, falling into his arms. A silly romantic picture. Irrationally it filled her with sadness.

'She was very lucky,' Yael whispered and again regretted speaking her thoughts.

Maksim stepped forward a pace. He lifted her chin. Yael closed her eyes; she felt his face close to hers. His lips were soft and she felt a pulse of excitement, of happiness, swell through her, as she responded to his kiss. And then she pulled away. Aleksei's face filling her mind. In the dim light Maksim looked at her.

'The father . . .' she said. 'The father of my child, he isn't dead.'

Maksim continued to look at her. He was

stood no more than a pace away. Yael felt a desperate urge to reach out and touch him. To have him take her face in his hands again and kiss her.

'The father?' he said. 'What happened to him?'

Yael shook her head. 'He's alive still,' was all she could say.

'Do you know where?'

Yael nodded. 'Towards Selo.'

Maksim nodded. He stepped back. Yael felt a small wrench in her heart. I'm lonely, she wanted to say. Hold me, she wanted to scream. She wanted to feel his arms around her. To smell his skin close against hers. She wanted to feel the closeness of another human being, the comfort of an embrace.

'It's late,' he said. 'You should get some sleep.'

She heard the sound of footsteps in the brush behind her. Anna emerged into the clearing, rifle slung across her shoulder.

'Yes,' Yael whispered, and ducked back through the branches of the trees, avoiding the look Anna shot at her.

28

Even out in the woods the festivals and holidays were observed. *Sukkot* was celebrated with particular poignancy, the makeshift shelters of the forest reminding them all of the small booths they had constructed on their porches back in the villages. 'So it has been and so it shall always be,' an elderly man commented. 'Once more we are in the wilderness, fleeing the evil oppressor.'

'But this time we have no Moses,' one of the younger partisans commented bitterly, 'and there is no promised land awaiting us.'

Maksim respected the routines and strictures of the older generation, without particularly participating in them. He never sent out partisans on the Sabbath, but neither did he join in the prayers led by *rebbe* Lazer. Some of the young partisans ridiculed the devout, but Maksim would always reprimand them, quietly but firmly.

After the incident on sentry duty, Yael retreated to her spot in the dugout. She slept badly that night, dreaming of Aleksei and then of Maksim, and confusing the two. She woke in the middle of the night, and lay for hours in the darkness, listening to the sound of breathing, the weeping of an old woman, an endless soft accompaniment to the snoring of *rebbe* Lazer, like a brook falling across stones. A child murmured and was quietened by its mother. Yael pictured Aleksei, and held her two hands over her belly. I will make my way back to you, she said to herself. I promise you I will be back just as soon as I can. She said the words over and over.

From inside her jacket she pulled out the photograph of Josef. It had become dog-eared and tattered. She gazed silently at his handsome face, the small, lop-sided grin, his open, relaxed stance in that little photographer's shop in Selo. And she wept for all that had been lost. She wept for her father and mother who she had not had a chance to say goodbye to. For the life that had been taken away and could never be restored.

★   ★   ★

She was concerned Maksim would misunderstand her behaviour, and resolved to apologise to him the following day. But Maksim had already left when she rose. He had gone off on a raid with three of the partisans Anna told her. He did not return for five days.

The weather had turned colder, and then as the weak light of day faded, it began to snow, large, heavy flakes that fell fast through the still air. At first the flakes melted when they touched the ground, but by late evening the forest floor glistened with a thin covering. By morning it was carpeted thickly. The snow was useful to the partisans, as it showed German troop movements up clearly. It was useful, too, to the Germans, leaving as it did clear markers to the partisan hideaways.

Yael had begun to grow heavier. The limited diet kept her small but, by the turn of the year, her belly was distended and her breasts had begun to swell. As she found moving about more difficult, Yael withdrew into herself. Often she would find herself weeping, and when Anna, or the young girl Esther crouched down beside her to offer comfort, she was not able to explain the reason for her tears.

'I'm not unhappy,' she cried to Anna. 'Quite the opposite, I feel full of life, of joy. I don't know why I am crying.' Anna seemed bewildered, but Esther nodded, as if she understood.

When finally Maksim returned, he continued to treat Yael with care and quiet affection. He kept his distance, however, and they were rarely alone. In the long, dark evenings, she wished he would come over and sit with her. She longed for his company.

As the endless, snowy days passed, she found herself spending more time concentrated on her body. She was hungry constantly, and her back had begun to ache as the baby grew larger and heavier. Occasionally when she moved around, she had palpitations and was forced to lie back down on her bunk, calming her breathing. She did not want to feel that she was a burden on the others, but found she had less and less energy. Often all she wanted to do was sleep.

Towards the end of February, Anna brought over to Yael the old woman who had first noticed she was pregnant.

'*Bóbe*,' she said, gently, 'what do you think? Say a few words over her.'

When the old woman looked at her, Yael was not sure whether it was fear or disdain etched across her face. She shied away now, not wishing to sit down.

'What is it, *Bóbe*?' Anna whispered.

The woman shook her head. She hesitated, as if unsure whether she wanted to say what was on her mind.

'There is madness,' she said, finally, her voice thin and cracked. She wiped some invisible thing from the surface of her skin, closing her eyes, as if she were better able to see this way. 'There is something about this child,' she said, her voice low, little more than a throaty whisper that was hard to catch. 'It is borne in darkness.'

Yael felt the hair on the back of her neck standing on end. Instinctively she covered her stomach with her two hands, cradling the bump, feeling the taut skin hard beneath her dress.

'Will it be a healthy birth?' Anna asked.

The old woman paused. She opened her eyes again and looked at Yael. The look was so frank and intense that Yael felt intimidated. She reached out an old and withered hand and moved away Yael's fingers. 'You must beware of any with the evil eye,' she said seriously. 'You must beware of Lilith. She will bring harm to the unborn child if you are not protected and constantly on guard.'

'Lilith?' Anna asked.

'Lilith, the first wife of Adam, formed from the sediments of earth, she is evil. Ever since the Holy One, blessed be He, took away her own children she has sought to avenge herself on young mothers.'

She reached into her pocket and pulled something out. Taking Yael's hand she pressed the object into her palm, folding the fingers tight around it. Gripping her hands, she threw back her head and began to mutter loudly. 'By this Most Holy Eye, I command all evil eyes to be gone, to depart and flee away from the wearer of this amulet and to have no power over her. And by the power of this most Holy Charm, the forces of evil shall have no authority over you, neither when you sleep nor when awake . . .'

Maksim, hearing the sound of the old woman's voice, glanced over. A small crowd of the elderly and the young had gathered around Yael's bunk, as the old woman prayed. He stood up sharply, knocking over the wooden stool he had fashioned for himself.

'What is this?' he said, coming over.

The old woman's hand shot out and he fell back, momentarily astonished at the authority of the gesture. She had switched to Hebrew. The words seemed to be coughed from the very back of her throat, spat out, harsh rushes of air. She pressed her hand down on Yael's belly so hard she let out a cry. Maksim stepped forward again.

'Enough!' he called out. 'Stop that!'

Everyone fell suddenly silent. The old woman let go of Yael and turned. Maksim seemed nervous of her. He glanced around. The faces turned from him, looked down at the beaten earth floor of the dugout. The old woman stumbled away across the room to the bunk she occupied on the far side.

'Are you okay?' Maksim bent down beside Yael, and reached out and touched her forehead, which was damp with sweat, despite the cold. Mutely, Yael nodded. She opened her fist and gazed at the simple amulet stuck against her palm. A tiny leather box tied to two leather thongs. She recognised the *kímpet-tsetl*, the childbirth amulet many expectant mothers had worn in the *shtetl*, blessed if possible by some *tsádik*. On it was written the words of Psalm 121. Maksim stood and walked away.

★ ★ ★

'What did she mean, do you think?' Esther whispered to her later as they lay together on the narrow bunk, the little girl's arm snaked around her large belly. 'When she said there is madness?'

'I don't know,' Yael said thinking of Aleksei. Their narrow, damp home seemed suddenly oppressive beyond bearing. She felt as if she had been buried alive. It was hard to breathe. She recalled Eva's story of how she had been buried beneath the bodies of the dead and of how the soldiers had spread the earth over them. Sitting up she pressed her head against the crude wood panelling of the wall. Her heart thumped and she felt faint.

'Get Maksim,' she croaked to Esther. 'I'm suffocating.'

29

The cold was startling. In the moonlight the snow glittered. A thick hard frost had crusted the top of it, so when Yael stepped forward the snow creaked and cracked under her feet. For the first ten minutes after rising from the sultry bowels of the earth, the cold was a relief. Yael stood for some moments, carefully opening herself to the sharp, brittle air. Her lungs stung.

'Wrap the scarf around your face,' Maksim told her, his own voice muffled beneath the thick collar of his jacket.

Yael did as he told her, wrapping it tightly so she had to breathe through the cheap cloth. The material was damp from her breath after only a few moments, and was frozen hard against her lips within five minutes. Maksim walked at her side, his arm looped beneath hers, supporting her.

'This is madness,' he muttered to himself. 'But then leaving you there is madness too.'

'Where are we going?'

'You need the care of a doctor, just in case,' he said, squeezing her arm. 'Just in case.'

'In case Lilith comes for me and the charm

is not strong enough?' Yael laughed.

'In case you need medical attention when you give birth.' Maksim's face was serious. Yael was finding it difficult to follow him. Her body was heavy and her feet unsure. The snow was thick enough to make walking difficult. Within two hundred metres she had grown tired and was breathing heavily. Maksim slowed down and took her hand.

'I'm not sure I am going to be able to make it that far,' Yael said.

'Don't worry,' Maksim reassured her. 'We'll take it slowly.'

★ ★ ★

The moon was little more than the sliver of a fingernail, but the clarity of the air lent it a vivid luminosity. Across the velvet dark sky the stars were speckled thickly, and the Milky Way seemed, to Yael, to form a celestial road across the heavens. It was dry and the cold burned her skin. The snow crunched beneath her boots. Beside her she could hear Maksim's heavy breathing. She was pleased to be out of the camp; its fetid, close air, the squabbles, the sharp stink of human waste, the coughing, the moaning, the crying in the night, the press of bodies, but she was not sure how long she could survive the cold of the night air. She felt vulnerable without the close proximity of the other partisans. She was also not sure she wanted to see a doctor. What she wanted, more than anything was just to retreat on her own to some silent place, where she could settle and wait for the child. She was not worried, not even at the thought of the pain, or the complications that might arise.

At the top of a rise, where the forest petered out leaving an isolated copse overlooking the surrounding countryside, they found a narrow shelter made from the branches of spruce. The young partisans had made it, Maksim explained, and used it when out scouting. At the back of the dark shelter they found evidence of nesting, and paw prints in the snow suggested a fox was using the shelter.

Yael curled up on the ground and Maksim covered her with a blanket he had been carrying. Despite this Yael trembled with cold. Her feet were icy. Her teeth chattered. After an hour, Maksim shook her. She had just dozed off for a few seconds and rose from sleep with shock. The cold overwhelmed her once more.

'I can't,' she wept. 'I can't go on.'

Maksim lifted her to her feet and guided her out of the shelter. She found it difficult even to stand, and Maksim was forced to loop his arm beneath her and half carry her down the slope into the woods on the far side. They slipped on the ice, and Yael could see Maksim was struggling. She prised herself free of him, and getting to her feet, walked on determined.

Dawn was imminent when Maksim grunted and, touching her arm, indicated a column of smoke that rose thinly above the ridge of a hill.

'The doctor's house,' he said.

* * *

Doctor Sonenson in the Selo *shtetl* had been a well off and respected figure. Yael recalled his half-moon spectacles, the fine cut of his overcoat and the smell of the cigars he smoked. He lived in a large house on the edge of the village, neighboured by the houses of the Polish merchants and businessmen. His reputation was such that many of the *goyim* in Selo called upon him, even though there was a Polish doctor in the village.

The house of the doctor Maksim led Yael to was not so impressive. It was a low wooden building with a dark shingled roof on which the moss grew luxuriantly. The house had once been painted a shade of blue, but the weather had washed this away, leaving bleached grey wood that was beginning to splinter. On the apex of the roof a small, thin chimney stood at an angle, and from this smoke poured into the clear morning air. There were no other signs of life. The small windows were dark and the door, in the small ornate porch, was locked.

Maksim rapped gently on the glass pane of the door. The glass was dirty and behind it the net curtains were drawn tight so it was impossible to see through into the dark room. After waiting a minute, Maksim strode around the side of the house and knocked on one of the windows, calling out in a low voice.

'Doctor,' he said, his Polish accented heavily. 'Doctor Wobel.'

Something stirred inside the house. A faint light glimmered in one of the windows and a moment later the door at the back of the house creaked open and an elderly man stepped out, holding a rifle.

The grey-haired man peered out into the dawn half-light, his hands shaking so the gun jumped in his hands and Yael was afraid it might go off accidentally.

'Who is that?' he called in a low voice.

Maksim stepped forward so he could see him. His hands were raised in the air, to show he was not armed.

'Doctor,' he said, 'it's okay, it's me.'

The doctor recognised Maksim, but he did not lower his rifle. His eyebrows rose a little and he half glanced back over his shoulder at the open door of the house. Yael, standing behind Maksim, saw a movement in the darkness. A shadow passed in front of the dim lamp and a floorboard creaked.

'Tomaz?' a thin voice called from inside. 'Who is it?'

The doctor waved the barrel of the gun at Maksim. 'Go,' he said roughly, waving back towards the woods. 'Go, quickly.'

Maksim opened his mouth to protest, but the old man raised the rifle. Yael cried out softly. Maksim turned and caught her arm. They stumbled back through the snow into the woods. Turning they saw the old man stood still in the doorway. A woman poked out her head beside him. They spoke briefly, before the woman's head disappeared again. Once inside the woods, Maksim doubled back, turning west; he led Yael around the back of the doctor's house to an isolated barn, the roof of which had half-collapsed.

'We can shelter here,' he said.

There were some missing panels at the back of the barn and they slipped inside. Daylight streamed through the half-open roof. In the corner, at the back of the barn, where the roof was more or less intact, a couple bales of hay had been spread on the floor. Yael dropped down on the pile and began to cry. It was the cold and the exhaustion more than the disappointment over the doctor. Maksim knelt beside her and held her in his arms. She clung to him, the tears wetting the collar of his jacket.

The sound of footsteps startled them both. Maksim sat up and reached for the pistol in his belt. He had cocked it by the time the old barn door creaked open and the doctor appeared. His glanced around and noticed them in the corner. Closing the door carefully behind him, he hurried across to the hay bales.

'Sorry, sorry,' he was muttering as he drew close. He eyed the handgun nervously. Seeing he was not armed, Maksim lowered it. 'My wife,' the doctor carried on, 'I don't trust her. If she knew you were Jews she would tell the Nazis.' He squatted down awkwardly and peered at Yael and Maksim. 'Now,' he said, 'how can I help?'

Maksim pointed to Yael. 'I want you to check she is okay,' he said, his voice still tight with wariness. He had pocketed the gun, but his hand hovered close to it. 'She is pregnant and the baby is due soon.'

The doctor nodded, his eyes taking in the large bulge beneath the thick layers of clothing Yael wore.

'How do you feel?' he asked Yael softly.

Light blue eyes shone out from a pale, kind face. His eyebrows were silver grey and bushy, while his hair was darker, flecked still, in places, with black. Yael nodded, unsure how to respond. Her body was frozen solid and she could not feel her toes or her fingers. Her legs ached badly.

'I'm fine,' she muttered.

He reached out and touched her gently. 'Wait here, while I get my things.'

'Do you think we should trust him?' Yael asked when he had gone.

'He has treated our partisans before,' Maksim said. He lit a cigarette and sat down in the straw beside Yael. When he offered it to her, Yael noticed his hands were shaking. When, a few minutes later, there was sound outside the barn, he jumped up and pulled out the pistol. Doctor Wobel squeezed back into the barn carrying beneath his arm a small leather case. He placed it carefully on the floor before Yael and rubbed his hands together.

'I'm sorry about this, but you may find my hands a little cold,' he joked.

Yael tried not to yelp when he touched the

225

stethoscope down against her skin. When she opened her eyes she saw Maksim standing behind the doctor peering at her. She found it hard to read the mixed emotions that seemed to cross his face. The handgun hung forgotten in his hand. The cigarette smouldered between his lips.

'Mother and baby seem fine,' the doctor said, eventually, pulling down Yael's blouse and looping the stethoscope, packing it back inside his case. 'The heartbeat is strong, the baby is moving around. It isn't yet in position. I would calculate she has another few weeks before there is any chance of her giving birth.' He stood up putting the leather case beneath his arm. 'She needs to rest and stay warm. She also needs to eat better than she has been doing, but then you could say that for us all. Beyond that, it is just a case of waiting.' He shrugged. 'There is not much else I can offer at this moment in time.'

'She needs to stay here,' Maksim said.

The doctor shuffled his feet. He ran a hand through his thinning hair. 'You know,' he said, 'it is not safe here. My wife, she is bound to discover her, and what if the Germans come by? There are a lot of troop movements. No,' he said. 'It is not safe.'

'Nowhere is safe, Doctor,' Maksim snapped. He bent forward and placed a hand on the doctor's shoulder. 'It is coming to an end, this war,' he said. 'The Soviets are pushing forward fast now. The Nazis are in retreat. When the Russians come who is going to vouch that you did not support the Germans? Your wife? You think her word will save you from being sent off to the gulags?'

The doctor shook his head, but Maksim slapped his shoulder as though a deal had been agreed. 'Nobody will know she is here,' he said, 'not even your eagle-eyed wife.'

30

'Is it true?' Yael asked, 'that the Soviets are winning? That the Nazis are in retreat?'

'They have been pushed back from Leningrad into Estonia,' Maksim said. 'It's only a matter of time.'

'Can you be so optimistic?'

Maksim shook his head. 'It's not optimism,' he breathed unhappily. 'It's inevitable.'

★ ★ ★

Despite his nervousness, the doctor continued to care for Yael over the next few weeks. He brought blankets out to the barn and, when he was able, provided them with food, mainly leftovers, and things his wife had set aside for the dog. 'He's getting thinner,' the doctor joked of the dog, 'and she can't understand it. I tell her it's worms.' The old doctor laughed.

Regularly, over the next month, Maksim made the journey back through the forest to see Yael. Each time he came, Yael felt he looked more drawn. Dark circles blackened his eyes. Sometimes, as he sat beside her in the hay, gazing out through the holes in the wooden wall, smoking a cigarette carefully, longingly, savouring every breath of what had become a rare treat, Yael noticed his hands continued to tremble.

'I'm fine,' he would state adamantly, if she asked what was worrying him.

The weather had begun to grow a little warmer. One morning, Yael woke to the sound of dripping. The next day it had frozen again, but the first scent of spring was in the air. That night Yael imagined her contractions had started. She panicked in the darkness. Hands clasped across her belly, face bathed with sweat, she imagined giving birth alone. The pains in her stomach eased off after a while, and when she awoke in the morning she could not say with any certainty she had felt anything at all, or whether it had not just been a vivid dream.

'Don't leave me,' she begged Maksim when he visited her the next day.

He stroked her face affectionately. 'When I come to see you here, it makes me feel almost normal.' He laughed. 'Pregnant and hiding in a broken down barn; this is our normality now. This is our paradise.' He laughed again, but this time he sounded sorrowful.

'I have to return to the group,' he explained. His eyes were bloodshot and his skin had begun to pale. Yael felt a pang of pity for him, for his concern, his quiet care. She reached out and touched the thick stubble on his cheek.

'We have joined up with another partisan group. We have more fighters now, and that makes some things easier. However . . . '

'Yes?'

He shook his head. 'It's nothing. I will be back soon. Take care. Do not give birth before I come back.'

'Absolutely not,' she smiled.

The days were long in his absence. Yael would struggle to her feet and pace around the barn. At dawn and dusk she would slip clumsily out of the back of the barn and wander slowly through the woods. The doctor visited her at least once a day to keep check on her. She tried to engage him in conversation, but he was jumpy and would not be drawn in. Often, while feeling her pulse, he would hear a noise behind him and leap up, startled, his eyes flashing in the direction of the doors.

In the empty hours, she would lie hidden in the straw, her mind freewheeling.

★ ★ ★

Maksim did not return the following few days. Yael watched the melting snow dripping from the broken roof tiles. The sky was huddled with heavy clouds and late one night it rained thunderously, and the water gathered in pools on the uneven beaten-earth floor. Yael was forced to retreat to a corner, where there was enough dry straw to lie on. It was cold and however she turned or buried herself, she could not get warm or sleep.

In the morning, as it began to grow light and the rain eased off a little, she heard a scuffling at the door. Sitting up, she saw a shadow pass through the entrance.

'Maksim?' she whispered fearfully.

The figure staggered across the barn and collapsed close to her.

'Maksim,' she breathed, crawling to him. He was sodden. His clothes clung to his almost skeletal frame. His eyes were dark and expressionless. His breathing came in short, shallow, spasms. 'Maksim,' she breathed again, her voice full of concern, 'what has happened to you?'

For the whole of that day Maksim slept in the dry straw in the corner of the barn. He shivered uncontrollably. Thinking of Rivka, Yael felt her heart lurching with fear. She could not lose Maksim as well. She undid the wettest of his clothes and then wrapped herself around him, allowing the heat of her large body to melt into his limbs, feeling the cold from him chilling the blood that ran through the engorged veins just beneath the surface of her skin.

When the doctor came in to check on her, his eyes widened seeing Maksim. Neglecting Yael he probed Maksim, felt his temperature, muttering bad-temperedly under his breath.

'I think he was worried you would die on his watch,' she said to Maksim the next morning. He had woken looking much better, declaring himself perfectly fine.

Maksim chuckled. 'A Jewish birth and death to look after! I can just imagine how he was feeling!'

★ ★ ★

Later he stood up and walked across to the barn door. He peered out, as if checking whether anybody was about, before returning to where Yael was hidden in the straw. He hesitated a moment before he spoke.

'I'm not going back, Yael.'

'You're not?'

'Things are changing,' he said. 'The Germans are being pressed hard. The Russians are on the advance.'

'But that's good surely?'

'Yes,' he said, squatting down and looking at his hands. 'This is good. However they will not be bringing a land flowing with milk and honey, Yael, Stalin is not the Messiah. I told you I was in trouble with the Communists before the war. If they catch me I will be sent to one of Stalin's gulags or shot. Many of our partisan groups will receive little sympathy from the Red Army. Once they have beaten back the Germans they will pick off their enemies, anybody Stalin can't trust. The partisan leaders will be carted off to some camp in Siberia.' He saw the look on Yael's face and nodded sadly.

'It's true Yael. Already . . . '

He paused and got up again, pacing back and forth.

'Bolsheviks are crossing the frontline, joining partisan groups, taking command, coordinating the efforts before the push made by the Red Army. I told you our group had joined up with another? I resisted . . . tried to . . . wanted us to remain neutral politically. I was given a choice: leave or be shot.'

He sighed a long and weary exhalation of his frustration and fear.

'But what will you do?'

Maksim was silent for some moments as if contemplating how he should answer, how frank he should be. He knelt at Yael's feet.

'More and more,' he said, 'I've been thinking about Palestine. Before the war I was against the Zionists, but now I think it's the only option we have left as Jews. We can rely on no one. Out here in the woods, we have shown we can fight. And look at what happened in Warsaw. No longer will the Jews sit idly waiting for their neighbours to attack them, no longer will we put up with pogroms and hatred. We will build our own state.'

He paused. Yael noticed the brightness in his eyes, the colour that had risen in his cheeks as he spoke. She was moved by his enthusiasm.

'I want to go to Palestine.'

'But what kind of country could we build?' Yael said. 'All we have left is hatred and fear. Is that any kind of foundation for a state?'

But she spoke only to hide the painful lifting of her heart. Hope. A future. Why did the ideas pierce her so sharply? Simultaneously she felt the child kick hard. She imagined travelling south with Maksim, pictured as a series of vivid vignettes a new life: sunshine, the sea glittering beneath the sun in Haifa. Then she thought of Aleksei. Of his child grown almost to full term in her womb. Thought of the quiet life they had enjoyed together. Of the intimacy she had shared with him. Of what that meant.

'Where else is there for us to go now?' Maksim argued passionately. 'For over a thousand years we have wandered, chased and beaten, murdered, expelled. No more. We will build a country of our own and never more will we have to cower in our houses in fear of our neighbours.'

'I'm sorry,' he said, smiling and laying a hand on her arm. 'I'm getting too excited. You look positively frightened.'

'No,' she whispered. 'Not at all.' She looked away and longed to hear him say, Come with me. A tear pricked the corner of her eye, but she brushed it away surreptitiously and busied herself, turning away from Maksim who had lit one of his few remaining cigarettes.

★　★　★

Later, looking out across the fields, she saw movement in the long grass and imagined it was a stork, that harbinger of spring, but looking closely she saw it was only a trick of the light. She thought of the storks that had nested around Aleksei's. She imagined them on their long route north now. Imagined herself to be one, making the journey south. Wintering in Jaffa, in the marshy plains of Palestine, along the reed beds of the Nile. Exotic, far-off worlds, beyond belief. She glanced round at Maksim. Felt a deep yearning. Tried to imagine such a world, such a possibility. Then banished the thoughts, afraid. Afraid that in fact life was possible. That there could be such a thing as a future without fear and war and death and hatred. That it was possible to build a new world, a new country where she may live and it not matter that she was a Jew.

'The father,' Maksim whispered late that night, faintly illumined by the pale moonlight. 'Will you go back to find him, when the Germans have gone?'

For some moments Yael could not think how to answer. It was the question she had been asking herself for weeks, months now.

'It's hard to imagine,' she stammered, finally. 'It's hard to imagine such a time.'

★ ★ ★

The contractions began that night. She had fallen asleep and woke late, when it was already dark. Maksim had gone out to find food. He had promised to be back by morning.

'At night you will be safe,' he assured her, 'it's the daytime when we need to be careful.'

At first she did not believe it. Could not trust it had actually started. For some minutes she lay still in the hay, her breaths coming rapidly and shallow, staring out into the darkness. Her muscles spasmed again. She did not have a watch to time them. They were far apart still. She knew the baby was not imminent. She tried to calm herself. Silently she prayed. She imagined what might happen if Maksim did not return. She had heard of girls who had delivered quickly, who had managed on their own, but she had heard too of girls who suffered endless hours of agonising labour. She remembered Leah Mishkovsky, a girl in her village who had died at the age of twenty-two in childbirth. She found herself imagining that now. What that meant. Her breathing had grown shallow again, fast and irregular. A sweat had broken out on her forehead. She tried to focus. She tried to calm herself.

As dawn began to break the contractions seemed to ease off. Yael sat up and felt her belly. It was tight and hard. She tried to move, but felt too heavy. By the time Maksim returned she had managed to crawl over to the bucket of fresh water the doctor had left and was wiping herself down. Dabbing at her warm face with some cloth.

'My contractions started,' she told him, breathless.

A look of panic contorted Maksim's normally calm features. He hesitated in the doorway. 'I'll get the doctor,' he said weakly.

As soon as he left, the contractions returned, doubling Yael up. Her whole belly squeezed hard and she felt a gentle pop and water pooled on the hard dirt floor of the barn. The contractions came strong and regular now, no more than a couple of minutes apart. In the moments when she was not paralysed, she shuffled over to the straw. Laying back she felt her body driving forward. She felt suddenly calm. There is nothing I can do, she thought, I am part of something bigger now. I just need to follow. She allowed her head to fall back against the straw, closed her eyes and gave herself to the next contraction, revelling in the power of her body.

'Come on,' she whispered, 'come my little baby.' And the reality of it struck her with full force then, as it had not until that point; that she was about to bear a child. That another human being was about to be born into the world. A child. Her child. Tears streamed down her face.

'How are you feeling?' Maksim's voice was soft in her ear.

She held out her hand and he took it and pressed it hard. 'The doctor is coming,' he said. 'It took me forever to raise him without waking his wife. I had to sneak into their room and shake him awake. Nearly gave him a heart attack.'

Yael opened her eyes as the doctor pushed through the door. He had dressed hurriedly and his grey hair stuck on end. He looked scarcely less calm than Maksim. He hurried over to the two of them and squatted down. Beneath his arm he carried his leather case and some towels. He glanced up at Yael and nodded.

'I had to tell my wife,' he said darkly. 'There is no way we're going to get through this in silence and her help won't go amiss.'

Maksim stood up, agitated. He reached inside his worn jacket and pulled out the pistol. 'If anything goes wrong . . . ' he stuttered, his voice tight with fear and anger.

'Maksim!' said Yael, before a contraction took her breath away. 'Put it away,' she breathed finally. 'Things will be all right.'

Maksim didn't look convinced. He glanced from Yael to the doctor, to the door of the barn, which stood ajar. Reluctantly, under Yael's insistence, he slid the gun back into his jacket.

The doctor's wife entered the barn just as Yael let out a deep groan. She looked around and her wrinkled face creased with anger. She carried in her hands a bucket of steaming water, but when she came over to them she shouted at her husband.

'And this is your hospital now?' she said, her head jerking back, indicating the dark, damp, cold barn. 'Get this girl out of here now, while you are able. Are you mad to be delivering babies in this filth?'

Her husband looked up at her nervously. The woman bent down and lifted Yael's skirt without hesitation. Maksim turned away. The old woman shook her head angrily.

'It's too late,' she said, taking over. 'The baby is already coming.' She stood and cast her eyes around, they settled on Maksim. 'Go into the house and fetch some clean sheets and towels. Boil more water when you have done that and bring soap.' Maksim did not hesitate to follow her instructions.

Yael felt her body beginning to push. She let out a scream. The doctor winced but the old woman was oblivious. She knelt between her legs, laying the towels she had brought firmly beneath Yael.

'It burns!' Yael choked.

The old woman cackled. 'It'll do more than burn little girl.'

Yael could feel her body stretching. It felt like she was splitting apart, as though her flesh would rip open. The doctor seemed to have recovered now and took over from his wife while she arranged the sheets Maksim had brought from the house.

'It's in a hurry to get out,' the doctor joked. 'Look, the scalp!'

Yael began to weep. It was not the pain, nor fear any more. It was wonder. Wonder at her own body, something she had barely paid attention to before. Something she had always felt to be inadequate, unworthy. Now her body surged with power. It was bigger than she. She felt suddenly huge. Her whole body pushed again, and she allowed the energy to surge through her, welcomed the excruciating pain. She opened her throat and bellowed like a cow she had heard in labour as a young girl on a farm in Selo. She gloried in the sound, in its animal ferocity. No more the still small voice, she thought fleetingly, between the contractions. Now, in this moment, I am the thunder.

'His head is out,' the doctor said, his voice tight with concentration.

Like the rapid rise and fall of surf, Yael felt her body collect itself for the next push. She worked with its rhythm. Pushed, breathed, squeezed and screamed with the cycle of parturition.

'It's stuck.'

'The shoulders are caught.'

'Hook your finger inside. Push harder girl, push harder now.'

Yael caught the inflection of panic in the old woman's voice and felt the first quiver of panic herself. She pushed so that she felt the veins would burst on her forehead, that her teeth would snap one against the other, that the muscles of her jaw would cramp. She felt the fingers scraping up inside her, felt the tug as she pushed.

While the doctor tried to hook the shoulder of the baby, his wife pressed down hard with the heels of her fists above her pubic bone, attempting to squeeze the baby forward. The baby kicked hard inside her belly, thrashed about. Yael cried, her voice echoing from the broken rafters of the barn, startling the crows which rose with frightened screeching.

She felt the sudden release. Felt the slide of the baby's shoulders suddenly loosened, its arms, hips and legs trailing, kicking even as it slid from the womb.

'It's coming!'

Yael's head fell back against the hay. Her chest rose fighting for breath. Her body screamed with pain, ached at every joint and in every muscle. She closed her eyes a moment. Gasped. Breathed. Opened her eyes and looked up at the doctor swaddling the baby.

'Is it okay?' Yael said, her voice trembling. 'Is the baby breathing?'

The doctor placed a bundle of material gently on her chest. Maksim, who had been watching from the shadows with a fearful look on his face, bent down beside her and eased Yael up. She opened up the towels to reveal the face of her child. Its hair was slick with blood and fluid. Its skin was grey and blue and red. Its tiny mouth opened and closed feebly. She opened the towel further, took in the little body. A girl.

'A girl!' she cried. 'A girl!'

The doctor laughed, wiping his hands. His wife stood grinning beside him, her pale flower-print blouse spattered with blood, hair hanging loose from the tight bun on the back of her head.

'Let the father have a look at his daughter,' she said.

Yael glanced up at Maksim. He flushed deeply, his neck turning dark above his collar. He said nothing though. He bent down and stroked away the hairs that stuck to Yael's forehead. He kissed her, and, reaching down, opened up the towels to look at the child.

31

'What will you call her?'

Maksim held the baby carefully in his arms, looking as though he feared he might break her.

'Chasidah,' Yael said quietly. 'Kindness.'

'A stork!' Maksim laughed, referring to the Hebrew word.

'A reminder,' Yael said.

'Well, little stork,' Maksim whispered to the baby, 'one day you will take wings and fly south, down to the Holy Land.'

Yael looked up. They were sitting in the trees behind the barn. It was mid-March and the snow had begun to melt. Buds were swelling on the trees and shoots had begun to thrust up from the dark earth. She said nothing. In the days following the birth, Maksim had disappeared into the forest. When he returned, he explained he had made contact with a Zionist group who were willing to help him make the journey to Israel.

'We can't stay at the barn long,' he said to Yael. 'I don't know how far we can trust the doctor's wife.'

The wife had been candid with Yael as she cared for her.

'He thinks he can't trust me, his own wife,' she grumbled. 'And, truth be told, if he had said you were here in our barn before, then perhaps I would have gone and told the Germans. You think that's terrible?' She glanced at Yael frankly. 'You want that I die for you? That the Germans should kill an old woman like me for looking after you? The law is the law and I do as I am told,' she carried on, pouring warm water in a large bowl to wash the baby. The steam rose, condensing on her wrinkled skin. 'If the law says I am to report Jews, then who am I to start arguing with the powers that be? What have the Jews done that I should stick out my neck for them? Did they ever stick out their necks for me? Or did the Jewish doctors take away our business? *Ei?*'

She shook her head and took the baby tenderly from Yael. She grinned as she gently lapped water over the child's legs.

'*Nu*, but you needn't worry child,' she said. 'I won't tell the Germans.'

Yael did not know whether to be moved or angered by the old woman. She watched as the doctor's wife deftly bathed the baby and swaddled her tightly in towels. Yael's body was still sore after the birth and it hurt when she moved around; she was grateful for the help. The old woman had given her herbs and teas to take away some of the pain.

After a week, the doctor told them it was no longer safe for them to stay on the farm. He told them he knew of another place where they could hide and early one morning harnessed up his pony to his trap and, spreading straw and blankets out on the back, drove them south, deeper into the woods along a rutted track to the hut of a woodcutter. The woodcutter was a middle-aged man, with thick arms and a face blunted by alcohol. He agreed to look after them for a while, and with that, the doctor quickly got back up into his trap and drove away, back through the forest.

★   ★   ★

They had been at the woodcutter's for only a couple of days when Maksim returned from one of his excursions excited. He pulled Yael aside.

'There was a raid on a village close to here,' he explained breathlessly. 'The partisans are camped not more than five miles away. Yael, I heard it was *Volk*, the Wolf.'

'You mean it could be Josef? My brother?' Yael's heart thudded. She felt suddenly faint as her knees went weak. She sat down on a crooked stool. 'We must go,' she breathed. 'Quickly, we must move.'

'You can't go with the baby,' Maksim protested. 'It's too dangerous.'

'Maksim, I need to see if it is Josef!'

He held out his hand to calm her. Kneeling down close he stroked her hair. 'I know how much this means to you,' he whispered. 'I will go. I will speak to him. If it's your brother, I will bring him back here.'

'But Maksim . . . '

'Hush now, think of the child,' he said. 'Think of Chasidah.'

★   ★   ★

The woodcutter said very little. When he was not working, he was drinking vodka which he distilled in a shed behind the house. Often late at night he would stumble about the small shack, knocking over the chairs and table, and Yael was forced to pick up the oil lamp, for fear he would overset that too and set fire to the building. She was afraid to sleep until finally he had drunk himself into a stupor and collapsed on his narrow bunk.

Chasidah was a quiet baby. She fed healthily from Yael's breast and was growing rapidly. Yael knew it would have been dangerous taking her on foot through the forest, but regretted letting Maksim leave her behind. She woke early the next morning and rose immediately, going out to see if there was any sign of him returning. The morning was warm. The air smelled of spring. The sky was clear blue and the sun, which had just risen, was so brilliant it stung the eyes.

All day Yael hung around the door, her eyes searching the woods, latching onto any movement, her heart rising, but by evening Maksim still had not returned. Yael began to worry. A five-mile walk would not take more than a few hours, even considering the difficult terrain. She tried to imagine scenarios that might explain why he had been delayed, but when she settled down for the night, a gloom had settled over her.

They were woken early the next morning by the heavy thrum of engines. The woodcutter struggled off his bunk and opened the door. He muttered an obscenity and turned to Yael.

'You awake?'

'What is it?'

The woodcutter did not answer. He stepped out into the dawn light. Yael followed him to the door, Chasidah in her arms. It felt as though her heart stopped when she looked out and a low cry rose to her lips. There were a number of German tanks squatted like ugly toads in the clearing at the foot of the hill. A group of four soldiers had hiked up the path and stood talking with the woodcutter. Yael withdrew quickly, but it was too late, as one of the soldiers indicated over the woodcutter's shoulder, pointing straight at her. The woodcutter turned and levelled his gaze at her. He motioned for her to come down to him. Trembling she stepped out of the doorway and approached the soldiers.

'Who is she?' one of the Germans barked, his Polish poor.

'Daughter,' the woodcutter said, enunciating the word carefully, slowly, as if speaking to an idiot. He wrapped his arm around Yael's shoulder and squeezed playfully, then pointing to Chasidah said, 'Granddaughter.'

The German nodded. He did not seem interested. His eyes scanned the shack and the forest beyond.

'Partisans?' he said then, in his broken Polish. 'You see partisans?'

The woodcutter shook his head and raised his shoulders in a loose, careless shrug. For some minutes the German soldiers conferred amongst themselves. Yael stood close, examining them. Their uniforms looked worn and smelled faintly of oil. The skin on their young faces was drawn, as though they were tired and hadn't eaten well. One of them chewed at his nails incessantly, so that they were bitten far down. Deciding the woodcutter knew nothing more, the four soldiers turned abruptly and hurried back down to the tanks.

As she watched them pull away she released the breath she realised now she was holding. She turned to the woodcutter, but the words escaped her.

⋆　⋆　⋆

Later that day a number of planes flew low over the woods. Russian planes, the woodcutter told her, when he came in from his work and sat at the table with a large tumbler of moonshine before him.

Maksim did not return that day. Yael stayed on at the woodcutter's not knowing what else she could do. Each morning she woke with renewed hope and would get up immediately and go to stand at the door and watch the sun rise. And late into the evening, long after the woodcutter had fallen into a drunken slumber and Chasidah breathed deeply, gently, in her sleep, Yael stood by the small window gazing out, hoping to see the sudden shiver of movement in the darkness, Maksim,

Josef, come back for her.

Chasidah was five months old when Yael was once more woken by the sound of tanks in the field at the foot of the lane.

32

During the summer and autumn the Red Army pushed forward vigorously, driving the Germans back into Poland. From the hills and forests close to the Byelorussia border, where Yael continued to hide in the woodcutter's shack, came the sound of heavy gunfire, the ear-piercing shriek of planes, the ground-rocking thud of explosions.

One morning the woodcutter led a pony and hay wagon up the track and piled the small amount of possessions he owned on the back of it, strapping them down tightly.

'We're going to have to move,' he said. 'Get out of range of the fighting.'

He lifted Yael and Chasidah up onto the back and silently they bumped down through the woods, into the lanes, to join the long lines of refugees fleeing west towards the centre of Poland. She looked back at the hut, hoping that somehow Maksim would find her.

★ ★ ★

Yael's clothes were little more than rags, and

Chasidah squirmed almost naked on her lap. Yael had tied an old patterned scarf around her hair, like the local peasant women, and kept close to the woodcutter.

The narrow lanes were chaotic, filled with farmers' wagons loaded with furniture and screaming children, quiet women and elderly men. German military traffic was often blocked by the refugees leading to angry confrontations and occasional fights. The evening of the second day, they drew to a halt behind a large cart, on which furniture was piled high: tables, chairs, chests and a wardrobe. The furniture had begun to topple sideways and the driver, a prosperous peasant who had no desire to leave his furniture to the Soviets, was trying to secure it with rope. In front of his cart a German lorry had stopped, with two more behind it. The driver of the first truck got out and remonstrated with the farmer, indicating for him to move the vehicle aside. The farmer swore and pointed to the sharp ditch that fell away from the road. For some minutes the two men argued in the centre of the lane, before a soldier leaned from the cab of the German truck and whistled to the driver.

Angrily the driver stalked away, whilst the farmer spat on the ground after him, and resumed tying his load. The engine of the lorry coughed into life and the vehicle leapt forward. The farmer shouted out, but the large metal bumper had already collided with the side of his wagon. There was a heart-stopping wail from the two ponies as the weight of the toppling furniture pulled them sideways towards the ditch. As Yael watched, the wagon tilted then seemed to halt. The farmer's hands flew to his head. The lorry revved and moved forward, toppling the wagon off the road. It rolled down the steep slope, the furniture scattering widely, the two ponies tangled in its load.

Later, they passed two bodies splayed out at the side of the road, bullet holes in their heads, the blood dried dark on the gravel.

That night they slept in the wagon, at the side of the road, amongst thousands of others. The sky was clear and the stars studded the darkness like jewels. Yael lay awake, Chasidah cradled in her arms and thought of Aleksei and Maksim. She pictured their faces, recalled her dreams, and felt only blankness. She could no longer feel hope, nor dare dream, or desire anything beyond that she and Chasidah would survive the night.

She hugged Chasidah closer to her, so that the baby's breath tickled her cheek. The faint beat of her heart thumped against Yael's chest. She recalled the Mayakovsky poem she had often read to Aleksei. She loved its passion, the energy and the violence of the love. She mouthed the words silently to the stars. 'Besides your love/I have no ocean . . . Besides your love/I have no sun, / but I don't even know where you are or with whom.' Oh Aleksei, she wept, my quiet *meshúgener*, my lonely stork, where are you tonight? Are you still alive? Do you still think of me? Do you know we have a child? A little stork of our own.

Early the next morning, they found the road once more clogged ahead of them. Children screamed in the road or stared blankly, fearful. Women huddled together. The workhorses looked tired and ill fed. An old man sat weeping on the back of a wagon, his toothless gums gnashing against each other. No one paid him any attention.

'What is it?' the woodcutter asked, climbing down from the cart.

'They're checking papers,' someone told him, indicating the road block. Yael climbed down from the wagon and stood close behind the woodcutter.

'What do we do?' she muttered.

He shook his head and raised his shoulders. 'We'll say we lost yours,' he said finally, and she could tell from his voice that he realised himself how feeble this would be.

He turned and looked at her. She saw in his eyes the olive darkness of her skin, her eyes, the blackness of her hair. He shook his head and looked away. Further along the German soldiers had taken a row of people out of the line. They stood by the side of the road, their heads bowed, and from the distance of a hundred metres, Yael could read the fear on their faces. She recalled the two bodies they had seen the previous evening.

Chasidah cried from the back of the wagon and Yael went over to it and lifted her out. Her milk had begun to run dry, she was eating too little and Chasidah had been testy and was growing thinner.

'They will know,' Yael said. 'They will see that I am a Jew.'

The woodcutter winced and Yael glanced around, but nobody seemed to have heard her. The refugees milled about the road, faces branded with hopelessness. Yael breathed in deeply. She hugged Chasidah close to her and decided. Turning to the woodcutter she pressed his arm.

'Thank you,' she said simply, not knowing what other words might express the things that needed to be said in times like these. The woodcutter nodded. He did not say anything as she turned and walked slowly back down the line of stationary wagons.

That night she begged food from a house in a small village. The woman looked suspicious, but took pity on the baby. The road the next day was clogged with more traffic. German lorries filled with injured, tired soldiers, defeat writ painfully across their faces. The soles of Yael's boots fell off on the third day and she proceeded barefoot, walking along the muddy verges, rather than on the sharp gravel of the roads. Frequently she slipped. She fashioned a sling from a shirt she found hanging from the broken window of a bombed out house and tied Chasidah close to her chest. The baby had grown quiet and lethargic and Yael worried at her slight frame. Late that evening she walked through a village that was completely deserted. The walls were riddled with bullet holes, and one house had been burned to the ground. It smouldered still, and the acrid scent filled her nostrils. She searched one of the houses but found little food. She drew water from the well in the back garden of one of the houses and boiled it over a fire.

A movement in one of the buildings frightened her and she rose and fled into the fields. That night she slept in a hedge, and the next morning before it had even begun to grow light, set off again.

There were soldiers in the next village.

Yael's head was light with hunger and exhaustion. Chasidah seemed to be sleeping. Occasionally, Yael would reach down and check she was still breathing. Her heartbeat seemed light. She kissed her head and begged her to keep strong. She recognised the village, having visited it some years before with her mother. It lay about ten kilometres south of Selo on the road to Augustow. The main square, a cobbled market place surrounded now by shattered buildings, was busy with traffic. Soviet army trucks, small tanks and motorbikes. Russian soldiers, large, oil-dirty men, many from the steppes of Mongolia, dressed in ill-fitting uniforms, cheap putties wound around their legs, loitered on the street corners or sat on their trucks laughing and joking. The few locals left there scuttled around with their heads down.

Turning the corner Yael bumped into a figure she recognised. It took her a few moments to place the narrow pinched face and the round glasses.

'You!' he said startled.

It was the brother of the partisan who had visited Aleksei's farm. For a few short weeks Rivka and she had stayed together in the woods with the two boys as they searched for a partisan group to join.

The young man took off his cap and wiped

his forehead with the back of his sleeve. He squinted at Yael.

'You're alive,' he stuttered, as though this was a surprise to him. 'And Rivka? Is she okay?'

It seemed so long ago, such a different world that Yael could barely connect the two moments in time in order to frame her answer. She shook her head. The boy nodded gravely, as if this was what he had expected.

'I met your brother,' Yael said. 'He was with a partisan group.'

The boy nodded again. 'We were separated,' he explained. 'I heard he was fine. You look bad,' he said then. 'When was the last time you ate?'

Yael shrugged. She felt suddenly weary. Such a desperate exhaustion she felt she could barely stand. He took her arm and led her across the square to a makeshift military hospital. Sitting her on a hard wooden chair in the entrance to what had been the town's theatre, he spoke to the officer at the door.

'Don't worry,' he said a few moments later, 'they will look after you.'

He had gone before Yael thought to ask his name. She wondered that she could not remember it from the days they had spent together in the forest. A Russian doctor came over and took Chasidah from her.

'What is her name?' he asked kindly.

'Chasidah,' Yael answered.

He raised his eyebrows at this, but took the baby away, carrying her with care. The hospital smelled of powerful, cheap disinfectant, and beneath that of death. She closed her eyes and when some moments later someone tapped her on the shoulder realised she had fallen to sleep.

'Can you walk?'

Yael nodded. She followed the nurse down the corridor and undressed as she was told in the stark, cold, tiled washroom. An elderly women helped wash her down and sprinkled her with powder. They cut short her hair and powdered that too, so that she stank.

'Lice,' they said by way of explanation as they cleaned her roughly. She was given a rough cotton robe to wear and shown to a bunk where she lay.

'Where is my baby?' she asked the nurse who had taken her pulse and temperature and asked her questions and listened to her lungs and ascertained that she was not carrying any infectious diseases.

The nurse nodded towards a door at the end of the ward. 'Children's ward,' she said. 'Don't worry, they will let you know how she is.'

* * *

As neither she nor Chasidah were sick, simply tired and malnourished, they were discharged the following day and told to report to the schoolhouse where there was a refugee camp established. There, she was told, there would be food and her papers could be sorted out.

'Jewish?' the officer at the entrance to the schoolhouse asked her. When she assented, he pointed perfunctorily across the road past a church whose bell tower was shattered, to a low building at the end of the lane. 'Jews over to your church,' he said with a sigh, as if he had continually had to clarify this issue that morning.

Yael was a little confused and stepped out nervously onto the road, crossing to the tumbled down Catholic chapel.

'Not there!' the Russian called irritably and pointed down the lane.

The building was a synagogue. Despite having avoided any kind of bomb damage the inside of the building was shattered. A fire had destroyed one corner, the windows were all broken and the walls daubed with paint and dirt. The furniture that had not been stolen, or used to light the fire, had been broken to pieces. She was greeted by two young men, members of a Zionist Youth Movement who were organising the cleaning up of the building. They registered her and

261

pointed her towards the far corner where she would be able to get some food. After that they would be appreciative of her help, they said.

Late that night the town reverberated to heavy gunfire. A shell hit the outskirts, and through the broken windows of the synagogue they could see the glow of the flames of burning buildings and the shouts of Russian soldiers rushing back and forward. The fighting continued throughout the next day, at some points coming so close they could hear the sound of light arms fire. The two Zionists went off to fight with the Russians and Yael took over the job of organising the tidying up of the synagogue, while formulating a plan of escape should the Germans break through the Russian line.

Yael was grateful that at least she and Chasidah had somewhere to rest and a small amount of food each day.

By late the following day the fighting receded again. The traffic through the town continued and the air was continually shaken by the sound of low-flying Russian planes screaming overhead. By late evening more refugees poured out of the forests into the narrow streets, growing confident in the stories that the Russians had beaten back the Nazis. The synagogue was soon busy with

Jews of all ages, though mainly young men and women from Koenigsberg, Vilna, Lodz, Bialystok, Warsaw.

In November, with the weather still holding up, Yael set off along the road north, towards Selo with Chasidah.

33

The traffic on the road into Selo was heavy. Military vehicles competed with farm wagons loaded with returning refugees. The bridge had been blown. Soviet engineers had built a makeshift metal replacement that shuddered and swayed as the traffic passed over it. The air seemed heavy and sullen. Much of the outskirts of the small town lay in ruins. Smoke still rose in some places and everywhere was the scent of burning.

Yael walked across the bridge clasping Chasidah tightly to her. Russian soldiers stared at her with lifeless disinterest. Locals scuttled around with their heads down, avoiding communicating with each other. Their faces were sunken with hunger, their eyes dark with bitterness. The market place was quiet; on one side a few people traded worthless goods off the pavement, on the other, in front of the police station a gallows stood from which two bodies swung slowly in the morning breeze.

Yael caught sight of an old acquaintance, an elderly woman of some wealth for whom her father did much work. The woman's clothes were tattered and her hair hung in loose greasy curls. Seeing Yael the woman's mouth fell open. Yael half-raised her hand in greeting, but the woman's eyes darted away. She turned quickly and shuffled across the broken cobbles, disappearing quickly into the shadows of a side street.

It was not just the old synagogue that had been burned to the ground, the church had suffered much damage too. A fire had gutted the insides and the roof had fallen in. Each of the stained glass windows had been shattered. Every bit of glass had gone, as if someone had systematically gone round and broken every last one.

Though few people lingered in the streets, apart from the Russian soldiers, Yael got the feeling she was being watched. She felt uncomfortable, and tried to ignore the glimmer of panic that was growing inside. She hurried across the square, her head low, avoiding the malevolent sidelong glances thrown her way. One of the vendors sitting on the corner, a man in his twenties Yael did not recognise, had spread out before him a range of items from old shoes, with soles split from their cheap leather uppers to a small seven-branched candelabra of the type found in Jewish homes. Yael paused to examine the trinkets, but the man looked up. His eyes took her in quickly. He let out a low growl, low enough that the soldiers might not hear. Quickly he gathered the stuff together into a threadbare blanket and disappeared.

The streets leading off the square were deserted. Here as elsewhere in the town the houses were in various states of devastation. Some fortunate ones seemed untouched, the paint still bright on the undamaged woodwork, whilst next door, all that stood was the brick chimney, teetering over the blackened rubble. Turning off Pilsudski, she hurried down Blacksmith's Street. Turning right at the familiar corner she ducked down the alleyway between Eli Koppelman's house and Michael Leizer, the butcher's, one-storey cottage.

She felt her heart beating hard as she stepped out onto the back lane, the small rutted road on which her house stood. What had she expected? She wondered, pausing, trying to control her breathing. Chasidah cried in her arms and she realised she had been squeezing her tight.

'This is *Máme's* home,' she whispered to the little girl, who opened her eyes. 'Where *Táte* and *Máme* . . . ' she stopped. Corrected herself. '*Zéyde* and *Bóbe*.' Grandfather. Grandmother. 'And Josef, uncle Josef lived . . . ' she whispered. Her heart wrenched. 'Oh God!'

she murmured. The pain felt crushing. The desire to run across the path and fall into her mother's arms. To hear her father's quiet voice. To see Josef. To know their home once more. 'Oh God!' she cried, tears flowing down her face, dripping onto Chasidah's cheeks, so that the baby raised a fist to wipe at it clumsily.

There was a movement in the window and Yael jumped. 'Josef!' she cried. She dashed forward. The road was dry, but the ruts were deep and she stumbled and fell and had to twist to stop the baby hitting the earth. When she sat up she saw the face in the window again peering out at her. A small, dark face. A woman with crude features, low sunken eyes and prominent cheekbones. A man appeared around the corner of the house and looked down at her. He too was small and dark. His clothes were tattered, and he was unshaven.

'Get out of here!' he growled. 'Get out you stinking *Zyd*!' He picked up a stone and made to throw it at her. Yael cried and sheltered the baby in her arms.

'No!' she pleaded. 'It's okay, I'm going.'

She clambered to her feet and turned down the lane towards the fields. As she went, she glanced back and saw he had come out into the lane behind her. She noticed the shoes, good shoes, leather brogues with fine stitching. Her father's shoes she was sure. The trousers too.

On the lip of the hill, at the edge of the meadow it was possible to look over the rooftops of the small town and see the extent of the devastation. The meadow itself had been churned up by the caterpillar tracks of tanks; an armoured vehicle lay half-submerged in the pond, its metal sides split open. Yael crossed the hill and hurried across the fields.

What surprised her as she walked around Czeslaw's farm, where she and Rivka had hidden for some weeks, was how close the distances were, and how short the walk. She recalled it had taken her days to make this journey before. It was beginning to grow dark as she mounted the hill towards the woods. She was tired and Chasidah was moaning, tired of being carried. Yael glanced up at the sky, trying to ascertain how long she had before darkness fell. The idea of walking through the forest alone in the dark did not appeal to her, but she was desperate now to make the journey, the last few kilometres that would take her back to Aleksei.

'Just a little bit, now,' she whispered to the baby. 'Just a little while and you will see your father.'

Chasidah's eyes opened and Yael paused.

Her little girl's eyes were large and blue. Yael marvelled at them. At the continual serious-ness of her small face. Even when she sat her on her knee and laughed and joked with her, the baby frowned in response. Yael stroked the soft flesh of her cheek gently.

'Yes, my little one,' she whispered. 'Your father.'

The word sounded strange on her lips. She tried to imagine how he would respond. She tried to imagine what would happen when he opened the door and saw the two of them there. She could not. It had been over a year since she had left through the open window into the night. She had dreamed of this moment for so long she could barely believe, as she set off once more, pushing through the branches of the trees, she would be back at the farmhouse just after nightfall.

She walked quickly. The baby was quiet, as though she understood the urgency of the situation. There was little other noise beyond the sound of Yael's feet in the undergrowth and her heavy breathing.

The sun had dipped over the horizon as she stepped out of the wood onto the lane at the head of his field. The sky was tinted pink and gold and the air was sharp and clear. The farmhouse was shrouded in the shadow of the low valley.

'We're there,' she cried softly to Chasidah. 'Here are his fields. Here is the house!'

She crossed the track, breaking into a run and stumbled down the path towards the farmhouse. Halfway down she stopped, her heart beating hard, and her breath coming in shallow gasps. No light shone in the window. He will be in the kitchen, she thought, and the memory of how she had first seen him, head bent over the table of that small room, the book open before him, filled her heart with love so sharp it felt as though she had been stabbed.

'Aleksei!' she called as she reached the corner of the farmhouse.

'Aleksei!'

She stumbled and fell, grazing her knees. Chasidah cried out. The door of the house creaked and banged and Yael jumped back to her feet, ignoring the sharp sting of her cut legs. Soothing Chasidah, with one hand, she hurried round the corner.

'Aleksei!'

A fox sprinted across the field towards the hencoop. Yael shuddered and turned back to the door. It stood ajar. She crossed to it. Should she knock or just push in?

'Aleksei?'

She hesitated a moment by the familiar wooden door. The darkness was falling fast and heavy. The moment, caught between day and night, was silent. She reached for the door, but felt suddenly afraid. She clasped Chasidah to her, struck momentarily with doubt. What if he did not want her? What if he did not believe the child was his? What if he had forgotten all about her? If he had been glad to be rid of her?

She paused, her hand suspended above the door. When she allowed it to fall, the timid knock echoed lightly in the small room.

'Aleksei?' she whispered. 'Are you there?'

Her voice was so faint she could barely hear it herself. When she glanced down, Chasidah's eyes were wide open, as if she too were on tenterhooks, waiting to see how he would respond. She pressed open the door. The kitchen was in darkness. Yael glanced around. There was no sign of movement in the fields. The forest on the hill was black now, devoured by the night. She stepped forward.

The kitchen was empty. The tiled stove cold. The fox had pulled open a bag of grain which had spilt out across the floor.

'Aleksei?' she called quietly into the darkened room. The house was empty. In the bedroom, the books had been pulled from the shelves. One of the windows had broken. The air was cold and damp. Nobody had been living there for some time.

Yael sat down on the edge of the bed. The mattress was damp; mould had begun to grow around its edges. She untied Chasidah and set her on her knee. For a long time they sat in silence, listening to the night, the brush of a gentle breeze in the trees, the cry of a fox, the silence of absences: his cough, his movements, the sound of the leaves of a book being turned slowly.

There, on the edge of the bed all the absences fell upon her. All the worlds that had been taken. All the lives that had gone. The stories ripped from books half-told. The poems strangled in throats. The towns unpeopled. Histories unwritten. The clothes that would no longer be worn by their proper owners, houses silent and falling into ruin, books that would lie unread. Bending down she picked up a volume from the floor. The pages were damp and one ripped as she opened it. Pushkin.

'Oh God,' she cried. 'Oh God how could it all just go?'

★   ★   ★

Yael woke early. Chasidah dozed still, beside her on the mattress. For some moments she could not be sure what it was that had awoken her. Sunlight streamed through the dirty window of the farmhouse falling heavily across the jumbled backs of the books that remained on the shelves. Chasidah suckled in her sleep. As Yael reached across to stroke the baby's cheek, she heard it again and sat up, straining her ears. It was distant and hard to grasp. The soft breeze carried it back and forth, so that as she strained, it came to her in gentle waves.

Her eyes were blurred with sleep, so when she peered out through the dirty panes, the hill up to the road seemed misty. She opened the window and hung out. The sound was clearer then. Singing. Children singing, together, as though it was a school choir. Picking up Chasidah, Yael ran from the farmhouse and dashed around to the front. They were walking along the lane, about twenty children, with three or four adults, one at the front, the rest at the rear. The words of the song carried down the slope, and it was clear now, and Yael could make them out. *Ani máymin.*

'*Ani maymin b'emuno shleymo b'viyas ham-oshíakh; v'af al pi she'yismaméya, im kol ze, akháke ley b'khol yeym she'yovey.* I believe with perfect faith in the coming of the Moshiach; and even though he may tarry, nevertheless, I wait each day for his coming.'

273

It was a well-known song. The prayer was one that Jews recited as part of their morning prayers. The lightness of the children's voices as they marched along the road in the light of the newly risen sun filled Yael's heart with unexpected but painful joy. She found herself following the song, mouthing the words silently, tears salting her lips.

Already the party had passed, moving along the road, away from Selo towards Grodno.

'Wait!' Yael called.

She raced up the field, slipping in the grass, which was wet with dew. The baby cried in her arms and Yael shushed her breathlessly as she stumbled forward. The party looked startled as she appeared. She recognised the look of instinctive wariness on their faces.

'Don't stop,' she said in Yiddish. 'Don't stop singing.'

Silently they stared at her as she struggled up onto the road, Chasidah bawling in her arms. She took up the song herself, half-laughing, half-crying, her voice hopelessly out of tune. A child, a girl of about eight years, smiled then hearing the song sung so badly. Kindly she broke into song, taking up from where Yael was singing. The others joined in. The young girl held out her hand and Yael took it.

34

The lights of the fires in the old market area, close to the railway station, flickered in the breeze. Wood smoke hung thickly in the night air. Standing at the edge, looking out across the ragged, huddled crowds, it was as though the world had stepped back a hundred years, Yael thought. There was a shriek of released air from a waiting train. From everywhere rose muttered voices. The children Yael had been travelling with fell silent. They shrank back instinctively into the shadows.

Yael stepped forward, pushing a path through the bodies. A commotion was stirring on the opposite side of the square. Groups of huddled refugees parted. Somebody shouted. Yael paused and glanced up across the heads of the crowd. A few voices raised a cheer. From the cobbles of the old square rang the clip of horseshoes. Yael's hand rose to her throat.

The horse was not a large one. From the distance she was standing it was possible to see how scarred and battered it was. It was the sight of the rider, though, that caught her breath.

The horse stopped in the centre of the square, close to the arched doors of Grodno station. Quickly, a crowd of ragged figures surrounded it. Behind the first horse followed another. A young woman rode it, her hair cut short like a man's. The crowds gathered. Yael noticed the Soviet soldiers stir uncomfortably.

She ran forward, tripping and stumbling over the missing cobblestones, eyes blinded by tears, Chasidah pressed tight against her breast. She had to fight her way through the gathering crowd.

'Let me through,' she shouted, banging against the backs of the men. 'Let me through.'

By the time she had pushed into the centre of the swarm of refugees, the riders had dismounted. The horses were little more than bags of bones, their hides disfigured. Despite this, Yael thought, they bore themselves with pride. The two riders were on the far side. Yael edged around, pushing her way to them. In the press she reached out and touched the edge of the coat of the man. He stopped and turned.

At that moment she stumbled and fell. Her knees jarred painfully against the cobbles. She held Chasidah tight, afraid for a moment she had let her slip. When she looked up, he was looking down at her. She felt her heart contract, then open with joy. His dark eyes were filled with wonder.

'Yael?'

She sobbed. Still on her knees she found herself unable to move. He kneeled down close to her, no more than a foot away. His hair had grown longer, his face more gaunt, but apart from that he had changed very little. He reached out and touched her. Stroked her cheek.

'Is it you?'

She fell against him. Felt his arms close around her. Her face pressed against his neck so that her lungs were filled with the rich pungent scent of him.

'Josef!'

He held her back. Gazed into her face. Took in the child in her arms, who was moaning again. He wiped her cheeks with his thumbs, spreading the wet dirt in thick smears across them.

'My God you are alive! And who is this?'

Yael opened up her arms and placed the baby in his. 'My daughter,' she said simply, 'your niece.'

Beside him the woman knelt down, peering over his shoulder. Eva. The crowd pressed around them. From somewhere she could hear the Soviet soldiers shouting, demanding the crowds disperse. Voices shot back at them in Russian. Yiddish. Yael gazed at her brother as he cradled Chasidah tenderly, his dirty finger tracing patterns on the soft, rosy skin of her cheek.

It hasn't gone, she thought, they did not manage to completely destroy our world. Here was she, and Josef, and Eva, and here in her brother's arms another generation. She reached out and clutched her brother fiercely, so that he was taken by surprise. She hugged him to her. She felt Eva's hand reach out and touch her hair.

'*The flame, perhaps, is not extinguished,*' she whispered.

Josef glanced up at her puzzled.

'Pushkin,' she explained and took Chasidah back into her arms gently, brushing her lips against the baby's. 'A line I read once from a poem by Pushkin.'

Acknowledgements

The extracts from Russian poetry quoted in the novel are taken from the website www.russianpoetry.net with the kind permission of Andrew Wachtel. The site is an excellent resource for those wanting an introduction to Russian poetry with Russian and English texts. I am deeply grateful to the renowned Yiddish expert Dovid Katz for his help with the Hebrew and Yiddish lines in the novel. Any mistakes or problems with the Hebrew or Yiddish are entirely mine, there was only so much Dovid could do with the truncated texts given him entirely out of context. I am also deeply grateful to Annette Green and Lauren Parsons for the wonderful editorial work that has immeasurably improved this work.

We do hope that you have enjoyed reading this large print book.

Did you know that all of our titles are available for purchase?

We publish a wide range of high quality large print books including:
Romances, Mysteries, Classics
General Fiction
Non Fiction and Westerns

Special interest titles available in large print are:
The Little Oxford Dictionary
Music Book
Song Book
Hymn Book
Service Book

Also available from us courtesy of Oxford University Press:
Young Readers' Dictionary
(large print edition)
Young Readers' Thesaurus
(large print edition)

For further information or a free brochure, please contact us at:
Ulverscroft Large Print Books Ltd.,
The Green, Bradgate Road, Anstey,
Leicester, LE7 7FU, England.
Tel: (00 44) **0116 236 4325**
Fax: (00 44) **0116 234 0205**